GHOST HUNTERS

Spirit Fire

SUSAN MCCAULEY

Publisher: Celtic Sea Publishing, 12436 FM 1960 Rd. W, Houston, TX 77065

ISBN: 978-1-951069-12-4

Formatted by Dragon Realm Press
www.dragonrealmpress.com

In memory of the firefighters, police officers, and all the heroes who lost their lives due to the events of September 11, 2001.
Never Forget.

CONTENTS

Susan McCauley

CHAPTER ·ONE

The remains of wood and stone poked through ash and broken glass like charred bones. They were bones, in a way—the building's bones. I sighed and took in a deep breath of smoke-tinged air. At least the coroner had taken away the victims. I didn't want to see them. Seeing their ghosts could be scary enough.

I walked over a scorched beam that had fallen from the ceiling, leaving a gaping hole open to the sky, letting the autumn sunlight illuminate the building's steel ribs. Tattered bits of a singed paper skeleton dangled loosely from a door, hanging lopsided on its hinge. Halloween was only a few days away.

"The fire marshal hasn't been able to determine the cause of the fire yet, but we're glad it didn't reach the Cabildo," said Frank Martinez, my mentor. "That museum is filled with artifacts." Frank was not only my teacher, but he was also a famous psychic investigator and a retired officer from the head branch of the Office of Psychic Investigation (OPI) in Washington, D.C. If it hadn't been for Frank, I would have been sent off to some boarding school for psychic kids, which would have been super hard—especially since I was the only kid in history to become psychic at the ripe old age of twelve. I was an anomaly. A freak. An oddball. And the accident that caused it all had turned my life upside down.

"Do you sense anything?" Frank sniffed the air. I knew he was smelling for something more than smoke and mildew.

I closed my eyes and let out a deep breath. I could almost feel the fear and pain of the people who had been trapped inside. Just a few days ago they'd been laughing, talking, alive. Now...gone. Accidents happened so quickly, but they could definitely make permanent changes. My heart ached for the people who'd died in the fire. For their fear. For their pain. For their famillies' loss. The ache in my chest was real enough, but I didn't feel any ghosts. Not right now. I couldn't feel the energy of what people had felt in the past; that part was my imagination. What I could see and feel and hear were actual ghosts; that was part of being psychic.

I tried to let my mind relax and opened myself up to the smoky silence of the café. Birds chirped overhead, cars rumbled past outside. The mouthwatering smell of beignets drifted in through the collapsed roof, reminding my stomach that Café Du Monde was just across Jackson Square and that I hadn't had breakfast.

Frank had promised me breakfast there today. With the increase in the city's hauntings and spirit activity since someone had released a bunch of ghosts at the local hospital, tourism was way down in New Orleans. And lower tourism meant we could actually have breakfast at Café Du Monde without waiting in long lines. That's just what I needed to shake off these cold, smoky feelings of loss. Warm, melt-in-your-mouth beignets. Delicious, puffy squares of dough smothered in powdered sugar. My stomach gurgled so loudly I thought the walls of the burnt-out building might crumble down.

"Focus, Alex. The beignets can wait."

I opened my eyes, gave Frank a quick scowl, then closed them again, trying to block out my gnawing hunger and the amazing smell. Still, I only heard the birds and cars, people talking as they walked past. I didn't hear anything ghostly. I opened up my senses further, trying to imagine them unfurling like a giant sail, billowing out around us. It's something Frank had been trying to teach me. How to control my "gift."

I went through my new mental checklist, which was recommended in the *Elementary Psychic Studies* book I was trying to memorize as fast as possible. Usually, kids are determined to be psychic or Untouched—nonpsychic—at age ten. If they're psychic, they spend the next two years at school studying Elementary Psychic Studies with the book. Not me. Nope. I was trying to cram it all in my head in six months or less. That meant I had to learn the history of ghosts since the Victorians had unleashed them on us—aka "the Problem"—as well as the meanings and uses of the Seals of Solomon and other wards and sigils. Then there were prayers for protection and to help spirits cross over. Ugh. There was so much. And Frank wouldn't let me rest until I knew it all.

First on the list for trying to feel out a haunted location: What do you *hear* from the spirit realm? Second: What do you *feel* from the spirit realm? Third: What do you *see* from the spirit realm? Well, I'd already sorted out the living sounds of cars and people and animals. I didn't hear any echoing voices or desperate wails, but I could come back later with my cousin Hannah so she could check for electronic voice phenomena (EVPs). She'd love that. And my best friend Jason would want to come, too, of course. He was still working to tweak the ghost glasses, or *specula spiritis*, that his new teacher, Madame Monique, had given him.

I shook my head clear of my friends. It was Friday, and I'd get to hang out with them later this afternoon at Madame Monique's shop, Solomon's Eye. I refocused and let myself open up as much as possible, flexing the newly healed tattoos on my forearms that would keep me safe from most unsuspected spirit attacks. I'd received not one, but two black-ink tattoos on my forearms when I'd become Frank's apprentice. The first was the Fourth Pentacle of the Moon, which defends the wearer from evil and from injury to body and soul, and the tattoo all kids receive when they had been tested as psychic. The second one is the Fifth Pentacle of the Moon, which psychics get when they start their apprenticeship with their mentor. The Fifth Pentacle of the Moon helps protect against all phantoms of the night that might cause restless sleep or nightmares. The protection was great, but still—two tattoos at once. Needles and ink. It hadn't been fun.

So, what did I feel from the spirit realm? Nothing. And what did I see? Again, nothing. Absolutely nothing.

I opened my eyes and shook my head. "I'm not getting anything. It's weird. There are usually harmless, stray ghosts hanging around, but here it's empty. Why'd the Town Psychics' Office want us to come anyway?"

"OPI is too busy, and the Town Psychics are still helping with the ghosts at the hospital." Frank scribbled a note in his work journal, and shoved it back into the work satchel that bulged with blessed salt, holy water, a knife, and an iron-tipped escrima stick. He never went anywhere without it. "I suppose they want to make sure that none of the victims from the fire stayed behind or that nothing paranormal caused it—especially since this is the third fire in the Quarter this week." Frank's eyes skimmed the shadows of the burnt-out room. "Are you sure you aren't getting anything?"

I shrugged, reaching out my senses again. Nothing. "Are you?"

"No, which makes me worried. You're right about the harmless spirits. There's usually at least residual energy in these old places. But it's like you said. It feels empty. Too empty. It's like...like a void." His dark eyes scanned the even darker room. "It could simply be because there was a new trauma here. It's possible any lingering spirits might have gone to rest because of the fire. I'm not sure yet."

The room was scorched; my eyes tripped over the remains of blackened, overturned chairs and devastated tables. I could kind of tell what he meant. I could almost hear the victims' screams. But that was just my imagination. Beneath the imagined fear and pain and loss I didn't actually hear anything. Ghosts to me sounded just as clear as if I were having a conversation with my dad. Right now, there was just a dreary sense of emptiness, like some black vortex had swallowed up all the energy in the place.

Just then a charred wisp of white cloth whipped around the corner where the counter had been, and the double doors leading to the kitchen flapped back and forth and back and forth.

Frank's gaze snapped up to the still-swinging doors.

"Did you see that?" I asked softly. The weird empty feeling left me, and now I was filled with the familiar cool tingle I got in the presence of a ghost.

"I don't know what I saw." Frank's voice was a low, coarse whisper. "But I see the doors moving." He looked up through the hole in the roof. The sky was clear and blue. There was a slight, crisp breeze. A perfect autumn day. "Could have been the wind."

"Maybe," I agreed. But maybe not. "Let's check." Even though he was an extremely experienced psychic, my abilities were even stronger. Frank was a Class A Psychic just like me. We were considered the strongest types of psychic because we can see, feel, and hear ghosts. Sometimes we can even smell them. Class B and Class C Psychics usually have one or two ghostly senses, but they aren't as strong or reliable as Class As. We still didn't know why my abilities were so strong; maybe we never would. When Frank could hear and see snippets of ghosts, I could have full-on conversations with them. I even had one at home who liked to hug me—or try anyway. Mrs. Wilson. The fat phantom who had done her best to be a mom to me since mine died in the car accident that had shattered my hip and my life.

Frank tilted his head in a gesture that meant I should lead the way.

I walked through the singed, swinging doors into the crispy carcass that had been the kitchen. Not much was left in here. Just charred blackness.

"The fire marshal said this is where it started." Frank flipped on his flashlight, swinging the broad beam around the dark, crispy room. The ceiling hadn't collapsed in here, just in the dining room.

"Makes sense," I said. I pulled out my headlamp, flipped it on, and adjusted it on my forehead. I liked having my hands free when I was working a case. That way, if I need to write something down, grab some holy water, or use my escrima stick for protection, I wouldn't have to drop my light to do it.

"And the people were found in here?" I asked, even though Frank had already told me they had been. It just didn't make any sense. The café had just closed for the night when the fire started, so the doors should have been open, and there were two large plate-glass windowpanes in front that the people should have been able to break through to escape. So, why had they been found dead in the kitchen? Unless the fire had burned too quickly...or unless someone—or something—had locked them in.

"Yep," Frank said, now standing over the massive black spot on the ground where the fire marshal said the blaze had started.

The room was silent and still and smoky. I could barely hear my own heartbeat. Maybe there was something here. Something other than the weird feeling of emptiness. I glanced around the room, searching for the charred, white wisp I'd seen. Nothing moved, and yet I felt as if eyes were peering at me from the darkest corner of the room. I shined my headlamp into the dark, but saw nothing except for a blackened, water-logged wall. Still, something about the quality of my light had changed. The beam was less intense, softer.

"Is someone there?" I called out, my voice falling flat in the shadows.

We waited. Listened.

A small exhale, a whimper of a breath hissed against my right arm.

My chest tightened like a fist and I looked down, expecting to see a ghost, but nothing was there. I could feel Frank behind me, still listening. Watching.

"Who's there?" I said, with enough confidence to convince my heart to slow down. "We can help you."

A gentle tickle, like the touch of a feather, breezed across my right hand. Goose bumps coursed over me. I stepped back and aimed my light at my hand all in one move.

Nothing was there.

Then a giggle. A little girl's giggle echoed from the blackened corner of the room and a sick, slithering sensation wound its way around my gut, making me want to puke.

My light bounced to the spot where I'd heard the noise. Nothing. Just the same strange, dull quality to my light as before. "Did you hear that?" I asked, my voice catching in my too-dry throat.

Frank was beside me now, shaking his head. "Nothing. But I can *feel* something here. It's watching us."

I rubbed the chill from my gooseflesh-prickled arms and scolded myself for being spooked. This is what I was training to do. And if I'd been able to deal with the murderous Mr. Wilkes and the crazy ghost priest and pirates, then I could certainly handle the victim of a fire, right? "I heard a breath. A laugh. Maybe a little girl?" I swallowed, wondering if she was just a lost little girl who needed help, or if she was a malevolent spirit.

According to *Ghost Hunters: A Psychic's Manual*, a malevolent spirit was a type of spirit that had died a violent death. They knew they were dead, but were so angry about it that they'd take out vengeance on anything or anyone. Malevolent spirits were serious business, and had to be dealt with by psychics immediately, before they caused harm to the living.

Frank gave me a nod. "We'll have to come back tonight once Elena's closed up shop, and then we can find out exactly what we're dealing with. This might be a good case for Hannah to use her EVP equipment on, too."

I wanted to argue, but didn't. Hannah was eager to use with her new EVP recorder, and Jason had a new gadget to test. I really wanted my weekend free to spend time doing fun things with my friends, but as a psychic apprentice, I knew I didn't get to choose my days off. Spirits were more active at night, which meant lots of late nights. And when we got called on a job, we went. No question. It was part of our "gift" as Frank called it, but to me it seemed more like a duty. At least my friends could come back and help me on the case.

"So why do you think they were trapped in here? The ones who died?" I asked, walking back to examine the freely swinging kitchen doors. "There's no lock and the front doors were still open."

Frank shined his light toward me. "That's what we're going to find out."

Chapter Two

With my belly full of beignets and my lips still sticky with powdered sugar, I wandered with Frank a few hundred feet from Café Du Monde to Elena's shop. The antique wooden sign swayed gently over the door, marking the entrance to *Elena's Paranormal Investigation Services*. She'd only been open for a few months, but the Town Psychics' Office already relied on her—especially with all the hospital ghosts on the loose.

Her office furniture made the place look more like an antique store than a PI office, but the paranormal gear that lined the glass storefront let anyone who peeked inside know she meant business. Sigils etched in the glass sparkled in the late morning light, making the glittery bats and pumpkins and witch in the window even more festive. Elena loved Halloween. She'd even managed to convince Frank to give us the night of Halloween off so Jason, Hannah, and I could go trick-or-treating.

Hannah's mom didn't really pay any attention to what Hannah did or didn't do; she'd left all Hannah-related decisions to our aunt Elena. As for Jason, well, his parents were worried when they first learned I was psychic. But after Frank and Elena explained how Jason could use his hunting *and* inventing skills to help fight the Problem right alongside me, they'd decided to let him—especially after Madame Monique swept in to let them know how invaluable Jason was. It didn't hurt, of course, that Madame Monique turned out to be an old friend of Jason's aunt.

Frank had scowled about trick-or-treating at first, but then Mrs. Wilson had puffed up like some sort of ghostly puffer fish and told him how short childhood was, and that we should be allowed to have fun on Halloween. I smiled, remembering Mrs. Wilson's delight when I'd promised to let her smell all my candy. Now that would be funny. She missed eating, which is why I guess she cooked every meal for us. She said the smell of food wasn't as good as tasting it, but that the aroma was better than nothing.

I yawned, hoping I could grab a nap before we headed back to the burnt-out café tonight to investigate.

Frank pushed open the door to Elena's shop, and the new chime she'd hung at the entry tinkled brightly. It was like a miniature wind chime with a brilliant blue Nazar Boncuğu dangling from its center. I'd seen one like it at Madame Monique's and wondered if Aunt Elena had gotten it there.

Elena was restocking warding supplies on the wooden shelves at the front of her store. The other shelves held blessed salt, holy water, and sage, along with a variety of God's eyes in blues, purples, reds, and yellows. She used to sell mostly paranormal investigator equipment, but now she was also selling more of the protection supplies everyone needed as well. The opposite wall contained everything a paranormal investigator could want: EVP recorders, EMF detectors, and a parascope that looked exactly like the one Jason and I had helped Hannah buy to replace the one that got smashed up on our case at Lafitte's Blacksmith Shop Bar.

"Let Hannah and Jason know there's a case tonight. Hannah may get some EVPs and Jason can try out the new adjustments he and Monique have made to the *specula spiritis*," said Frank, setting his work satchel down beside the front counter and helping Elena finish stocking the salt.

"I'll call the school now and let the kids know to get some sleep before meeting us at seven." Elena wiped the dust from her hands onto her jeans and went behind the counter to make the call. "Solomon's Eye, right?" Elena asked.

Frank nodded. "Solomon's Eye."

The phone rang before Elena could even pick it up to call school. "Hello." She gave Frank an exasperated expression that said she'd call just as soon as she was off the phone. Then, suddenly, her face changed from exasperated to concerned as she listened to whomever was on the other end. "I understand. Yes. Very serious. Just a moment, please, and I'll see what I can do." She held the receiver to her chest so the person on the other end wouldn't be able to hear.

"What's the problem?" As usual, Frank was calm.

"It's the hospital again. The spirit of that psychiatric patient we couldn't contain is causing a ruckus. The Town Psychics' Office is requesting us because the local OPI officers are on another fire case."

Frank's brows cinched up when he heard the word fire. "We ought to go to the new fire case. Make sure it's not related to the others."

"You know we can't go barging into an OPI case without an invitation. If we do that, it will be the end of my already delicate relationship with them." She clung to the phone, still waiting for his answer.

"Right. And with Gallows in charge, he definitely won't welcome me there," Frank scowled. He used to be high up in the Office of Psychic Investigation and could do almost anything he wanted, but now the new head of OPI's New Orleans office didn't like him and made him ask permission for everything. I still didn't know why Mr. Gallows didn't like Frank. I did know that Mr. Gallows gave me the creeps. If that guy was going to be at the hospital, I was totally fine not going there. Finally, Frank pulled the appointment book from his leather work satchel, flipped it open, and skimmed the ledger. "What about Tuesday for the hospital?"

Elena spoke to the person on the phone, and I swear I could hear the voice on the other end rise a decibel. "Please calm down, ma'am. Let me talk to him." She held the phone back to her chest. "What about tonight?"

"Tonight?" I yelped, half worried Frank would send me back to the café on my own and half hopeful we'd reschedule tonight's job so I could have some Untouched fun with Jason and Hannah.

Frank shook his head, but Elena already had the phone back to her ear. "We have to go, Frank," she whispered with a sort of desperation I'd never seen from Elena before. She looked at me, then back to Frank. "The spirit is literally scaring people to death. He's in the cardiac ward. He's already given two patients heart attacks. Both were fatal."

"In Solomon's name," Frank hissed, rolling his head back, eyes to the ceiling. "Fine. Tell them we'll go tonight. But they need to be prepared for a long one."

Elena got back on the phone to set up the details, but I was too worried to listen. "So, we're just going to go back to the café tomorrow then, right?" I asked, more with hopeful relief than excitement for a night off. The last time I'd been given a solo case, I'd nearly cost Jason his life.

Frank set down his appointment book, stood in front of me, and put his hands on my shoulders.

Uh-oh. This couldn't be good.

"*Divide et impera*. Do you remember what that means?"

My brain scrambled to reach back into our Latin lessons, just one of many subjects I was trying to cram into my brain. "Um, to divide and..." Latin wasn't my strongest subject. Talking to ghosts was.

"Divide and conquer. Julius Caesar. You should remember that one." He patted me on the shoulder and gave me a small smile. "One of the good things about having an apprentice is that's what we can do. Divide and conquer. So, no. We're not going to go back to the café tomorrow night. You've got your team now. So, I want you to take Jason and Hannah with you to the café to figure out what's going on there. You don't have to cross anyone over. Just figure out what type of haunting it is, and then Elena and I can help."

A sick feeling twisted around my gut. "But I thought I wasn't supposed to take another case alone until I'm a 'full apprentice,'" I said, quoting Frank's words from after my first, and last, solo case.

Frank released my shoulders and narrowed his eyes. He hated it when I used his words against him. I grinned. Maybe I'd won. "It's not a hard-and-fast rule," he said. "It's a general policy to keep apprentices out of trouble."

I opened my mouth to protest, but Frank held up his hand and kept going. "You're as good as done reading *Elementary Psychic Studies* and your psychic skills are stronger than any apprentice I've ever seen. Plus, you have a team, which most apprentices don't have. Besides, there are more cases than all of us can handle. Remember, *divide et impera*."

"Right," I sighed. "Divide and conquer. But what if something happens like last time?"

"I doubt you'll run into a couple of pirates and a priest," Frank half laughed, his attempt at a bad joke.

"No. But I don't want to put Jason and Hannah in danger if I can't handle it." I shoved my hands deep into my pockets, nervously picking at the loose strings in there. I was still mad at myself for making Jason stay with me at the pub to cross over a couple of pirates and a priest in the middle of a hurricane. So stupid.

"You handled it last time." Frank picked up his work satchel and secured his appointment book inside, as if this entire conversation was one we had daily.

"But I almost didn't handle it. I almost got him killed." There. I said it.

"This business is full of risks, Alex. It's full of close calls. Full of almosts. But the important thing is that you *did* handle it. You saved Jason. You cleared that bar of spirits and helped those ghosts find peace. You're learning, and that's exactly what you're supposed to do as an apprentice."

"But—"

Frank slung his bag across his shoulder. "Hannah and Jason each have the tattoo that Monique designed. That will give them both more protection than any other Untouched. And I'll make sure Elena stocks them up on holy water and salt." He jerked his thumb toward the door. "You'll be fine. Now let's go home and get some sleep before the case tonight. I have a feeling we're going to need it."

A springy bounce jolted me awake as Mrs. Wilson's large bottom bumped me with a chilly nudge through the sheets. I groaned, not wanting to open my eyes. It felt like I'd only fallen asleep five minutes ago. "What time is it?"

"It's nearly six o'clock in the evening. You need to get *up*.... Get *up*.... Get *up* and eat!" Mrs. Wilson bounced each time she said "up," and I could sense the smile on her face. What was she so excited about?

I groaned again and pulled a pillow over my head.

Merow.

My ghost cat, Onyx, who'd sort of become my cat after the case at Lafitte's Blacksmith Shop Bar, walked up my legs and settled on my chest with a rumbling purr. Onyx was soft and cool and comforting. But Mrs. Wilson. She was freezing. Every time she touched me it was like I'd been shoved into a freezer.

"Get up, Alex!" Mrs. Wilson fluffed the sheet up over me, sending a glacial wave across my skin.

"O-kay," I groaned, tossing the pillow from my head and opening my eyes.

Mrs. Wilson was standing over me, a huge grin on her round, semi-translucent face. "Oh, good! I can't wait for you to try my new gumbo recipe. It's got chicken and sausage and rice."

Gumbo? She'd woken me up for gumbo? I glanced at the clock beside my bed. It was the windup alarm clock I'd brought from home. Mom and Dad hadn't allowed us to have electric clocks. Mom had always worried about ghosts getting in through the electrical currents. My heart gave a painful twist at the thought of Mom. She'd been gone for five months now. Dead. That's how long it had been since the accident. I hadn't cried about it in a while, but I still missed her—even though I knew she was in a better place. I suppose that was one good thing to come out of my being psychic—I'd had the chance to see Mom one last time when I'd helped the Wilkeses cross over. Dad had seen her, too. It was because of that, I think, that Dad finally supported me being psychic. Even if he didn't like it.

"Come on, sleepyhead." Mrs. Wilson yanked away my covers.

"Hey!" I yelped, covering myself back up. "I'm in my underwear." My purple ones. Nothing wrong with purple, and since I wore black shirts most of the time, it was nice to get a flash of color every once in a while. Not that Mrs. Wilson needed to see it!

She chuckled and tossed me a pair of clean jeans. "Well, get dressed then, and come eat some of my delicious gumbo. Then you'll be ready for your job tonight. Full stomach. Nice and warm." Then she disappeared through my bedroom wall and into the kitchen.

Onyx purred. I rolled my eyes. Mrs. Wilson had made it her job to act as a mother to me since mine had passed on. I knew she meant well, but I would rather have had an extra fifteen minutes of sleep than a bowl of gumbo. Holding the jeans Mrs. Wilson had tossed me, I grabbed clean underwear—camo ones—and a fresh T-shirt and headed to the shower.

The warm water felt so good on my tight shoulders and still-aching hip. I watched as the water rolled over the fresh scar that curved its way around my hip. A twelve-year-old with a full hip replacement. Not fun. But I was thankful I could still walk—even if I'd never play sports again. Not that there was much time for sports with my psychic studies. Although Frank was making me learn some basic martial arts with iron-tipped weapons called escrima sticks to help protect myself against malevolent spirits.

Merow.

Onyx slithered around the back edge of the tub, carefully skirting the water, and leapt onto the small windowsill that peered out onto the street. Thankfully it was only eye level, or any onlookers would get an eyeful.

"Can you even feel the water?" I asked, flicking a few droplets at him from my fingertips.

Merow. He flipped his tail, looking totally annoyed, but didn't move.

"Okay. I guess not liking water is a cat thing." I grinned and scratched him behind the ears. I couldn't feel his fur exactly, but I was rewarded with a soft, cool sensation. He meowed again and immediately started licking the spot I'd touched.

I shook my head with a laugh, turned off the water, and climbed out of the shower. I towel dried my hair, then wiped the steam from the mirror and studied my appearance. Same spiky blond hair. Same blue eyes. But I was getting older. Maybe it was because of all the ghosts. Or maybe it was because I was approaching thirteen. I had no idea except that all my clothes seemed to be shrinking.

"Gumbo?" Mrs. Wilson poked her head through the bathroom wall announcing food.

If it hadn't been so startlingly creepy and I hadn't been standing there naked, I would have laughed at her translucent, disembodied head poking through my bathroom wall. Instead, I screamed, "Get out!" I whipped the towel around my waist so fast I nearly tripped myself.

"It's not like I didn't have a son," she cackled. "Now, get your pants on and come out here and eat some gumbo. It's chicken and sausage. Delicious!"

The gumbo was good. Maybe not stick-your-head-through-my-bathroom-wall-while-I'm-naked good, but it was good. Belly full and body suitably warm, I grabbed my freshly packed work satchel—a roomy, brown leather bag filled with everything a psychic investigator could need—and headed downstairs to Madame Monique's shop with Frank.

Our two-story orange brick building was a combination apartment and storefront. Frank and I lived upstairs, and Madame Monique lived below us in the apartment-shop where she ran her occult business. The sign out front was painted black, and the gold lettering read *Solomon's Eye*. It had a bright blue eye for the first "o" in King Solomon's name and hung from wrought-iron posts, illuminated by the flickering gas lamps nearby.

Frank led the way through the yawning front doors, and guided us to the spot at the back that Hannah, Jason, and I usually claimed as our own. Elena and Hannah were already there, and instead of our usual table, Elena had commandeered a second. Both were scooted together and were filled with two sets of paranormal investigator equipment: EVP recorders, electromagnetic field detectors, sea salt, sage, and holy water.

"Where's Jason?" I asked as Frank and I set our bags down on nearby wrought-iron chairs. Jason usually rode with Hannah and Elena if they were coming this way. When he came on his own after school, he rode his bike. I was only about a fifteen-minute bike ride from home, but sometimes it felt like a thousand miles. I hadn't seen Dad in weeks.

Hannah tilted her head toward the counter and the double doors that led into the workshop. Madame Monique said it was strictly off-limits and never let anyone back there—except Jason, whom she'd take on as her apprentice. Jason had told me it was wicked cool. Loads of herbs and crystals and gears. Madame Monique appreciated psychics, just like she appreciated PIs and their electronic equipment, but she said, "I'm not psychic and I don't like electronics." So she, and now Jason, were creating their own methods of helping us deal with the Problem. By combining ancient African and Haitian magic, prayers, wards, herbs, and their own engineering ingenuity, Madame Monique and Jason were working to create nonelectrical mechanisms and charms to battle ghosts. I'd never seen Jason happier.

"You ready to go, Frank?" Elena flipped off her EVP recorder and placed it in her gun-metal gray investigator kit beside the EMF detector, then secured the lid.

"I want to cover a few things with Alex, Hannah, and Jason before we go." Frank nodded toward the back of the shop where Jason was hidden away with Madame Monique.

"There's been another attack." Elena's cheeks were pale. "The patient's off life support, but is still in ICU. We need to get there to help sort this out."

"Right." Frank turned a grim face toward me and Hannah. "Alex, I'll let you brief Hannah about what we found at the café earlier today. You can fill in Jason later. Just be careful and remember you don't have to cross anything over."

"We won't do anything we can't handle without you." Hannah smiled sweetly, then locked her own PI equipment up in its metal case.

I knew she was thrilled about going on another case without adults. She wanted to capture the best EVP and prove to the world that paranormal investigators could help with ghosts just as much as psychics.

"Hannah..." Elena's warning words made Hannah bite her lip and drop her eyes. "I know you're excited," she smiled, her voice lightening. "But be careful. Use your equipment, but remember you're there to help each other and keep each other safe."

"I will, Aunt Elena." Hannah patted the top of her PI case like an old friend.

Elena gave her a hug. "Good. I know you've been wanting to test out the EVP 3K. Maybe you'll catch something really good."

"I hope so!" Hannah smiled.

"Alex." Frank nodded for me to join him by an herb-encrusted shelf. The air was tinged with sage and lavender and myrrh. It was so pungent my nose tingled and my eyes watered. Whatever Madame Monique had for sale in this place was some strong stuff.

Frank coughed and batted away the bunch of dried lavender that poked him in the head. "I was looking over your Elementary Psychic Studies work. You're almost done, and you're doing well. So, think of this case as a sort of test. If you figure out what's going on in that café and finish up your work in there, you'll be done with the basics and I can sign off on you as a full apprentice."

Me? A full Apprentice Psychic in what normally took kids two years? All in a few months? Was he nuts? And why did I feel so excited about it?

But I was very excited. I couldn't wait to get my OPI Apprentice Psychic card. I found myself grinning. Just a month ago, I would have been totally disturbed at the idea. Now, I was all in. I had this gift to see and hear ghosts, so I was going to use it to the best of my abilities— even if I still didn't really know what I was doing.

"You're talented, Alex. You're smart. You're old enough. Just stay calm and have a plan before you act." Frank gave me an out-of-character fatherly wink. "You can do this."

Before I could respond, he walked back to the wrought-iron chair, picked up his bag, slung it over his shoulder, and headed to the front door. "Alright, Elena. Let's go and sort out this psychotic ghost."

Susan McCauley

CHAPTER THREE

Five minutes had passed since Frank and Elena left, and Hannah was nearly jumping out of her skin with impatience. Her bouncing almost reminded me of Mrs. Wilson—if Mrs. Wilson were a skinny, brown-haired girl with enormous glasses.

"What are they doing back there?" She stomped a foot and glanced at her WardWing. The WardWing was a great watch. Its hands looked like miniature wings, and the Seals of Solomon and other protection sigils were interspersed throughout the numbers. It wasn't as secure as my Spellguard, which is the super-cool watch Mom got me the last time she presented at OPI Headquarters in Washington, D.C. The Spellguard was supposed to be the safest electronic watch on the planet, with sigils inscribed on every gear and battery—sort of like mosquito repellent, but for ghosts. They didn't always work, but they still helped keep most of them away. My Spellguard had a special, nearly invisible seal on the face. And the numbers glowed in the dark. It was the same watch that every Paranormal Cybersecurity Squad officer wore, and I loved it. Still, Hannah's WardWing was awesome.

WardWing, Inc., had never had a traveler ghost reported jumping a ride on one of their timepieces either.

"We need to get going. I'd like to get there and set up before it's pitch-black outside." I looked out the thick, wavy glass of the shop windows, peering past the grinning jack-o'-lanterns Madame Monique had lit in the windowsills. "The sun's already set. We really need to go." I stood up and took three steps toward the double doors that marked Madame Monique's laboratory. "Jason!" I called, but stopped just short of the counter.

The doors swung open and Jason stepped out wearing the steampunk-looking ghost goggles that Madame Monique had let him use for our pirate case at Lafitte's Blacksmith Shop Bar. Except the goggles had changed. They still had one thick lens and another telescoping lens with strange sigils etched into the iron and brass, but now, just above the lenses themselves were bright, glowing blue lights.

I gaped at him. "Do those things have batteries?"

Grinning widely, he came around the counter, flipped a little switch that caused a tiny brass door on the bridge of the goggles to slide over the lights, making them go out, then removed the goggles from his head. "Nope. No electronics."

"We don't want to risk any entities using the electricity to corrupt the device." Madame Monique stepped out quietly behind him, a glint of pride in her eyes. "The lights were Jason's idea."

"You usually need a headlamp, you know? And if I've got these on, I can't really fit a lamp on my head, too, and I might need my hands free to help out. So, we added lights." He handed me the *specula spiritis*.

I studied the little slide door they'd built into the goggles and toggled it back and forth. Light on. Light off. Light on. Light off. "Bioluminescence?" I asked. Had they stuck some sort of biological organism in there?

"Nope." Jason grinned even wider. "No living things. It's diphenyl anthracene and hydrogen peroxide. When they mix, it causes an exergonic reaction. It's chemistry!" Invention, creativity, science. Jason was totally in his element—especially since he could use it all to hunt ghosts. He'd loved to go hunting with his dad. Now, instead of hunting animals, he could hunt ghosts with me.

"It's also got a bit of magic." Madame Monique gave us a sly smile. "So the light lasts for days instead of hours."

"Then how do you change it out?" Hannah was now standing beside me studying the altered glasses like they were a new gadget for her to explore.

"There's a little plastic vial that goes right here." Jason showed us a tiny door that opened so you could slide the vial in and out. "If the light's been used for more than three days, you just remove the old vile, and pop in a new one. To activate it you have to crack the tiny glass capsule inside."

"Sort of like a glow stick?" I asked.

"Exactly like a glow stick." He slid the *specula spiritis* into their case. It was a brown leather pouch with a long strap, sort of like a binocular case that was etched with the protective Seals of Solomon.

"And magic makes it last longer?" Hannah asked, with a voice that said she couldn't wrap her mind around a light-up device with no electronics.

"Certain sigils," Madame Monique whispered. "It's proprietary information, yes, *mon kè*?" she said to Jason with a wink.

Hannah grinned at the Haitian term of affection Madame Monique used for Jason.

"Come now, children. Have some Green Ghost before you go."

Jason made a "yuck face" at me that Madame Monique couldn't see, and I tried not to laugh. Green Ghost was a special, off-the-menu drink Madame Monique made for ghost hunters, psychics, and PIs alike. The shatterproof glass bottles were filled with green tea and iron. The caffeine in the green tea helped keep us awake, and the iron helped ward off spirits. It tasted nasty, but it worked.

After Madame Monique had checked to ensure we were all wearing our protective Nazar Boncuğu amulets, we packed up our gear and were off. I had my satchel, which was standard-issue for psychics and contained sea salt, holy water, myrrh, a spade, a knife, a crowbar, a rope, a notepad and pencils, a flashlight, a battery-operated headlamp with manufacturer-inscribed Seals of

Solomon, my copy of *Ghost Hunters: A Psychic's Manual*, and my iron-tipped escrima stick. Hannah had her case of PI equipment, and Jason had the *specula spiritis*. We all carried extra holy water and sea salt—just in case.

It was less than half a mile from Solomon's Eye to the site of the investigation. We walked down Chartres Street most of the way, enjoying all the Halloween decorations and costumes. We walked past doorways painted with skulls, porches decked out with zombies, and cackling jack-o'-lanterns with grins glowing yellow-orange in the night. There was even one storefront filled with a ghostly jazz band: skeletons dressed in white sheets holding tubas and trumpets and chains.

The streets were usually packed with tourists this time of year, but with the recent burst of malevolent spiritual activity, it was a tad bit slower than usual. Still, there were loads of hardcore Halloween fans that had come to New Orleans despite the ghosts—or maybe because of them.

A few people passed by dressed like flashy skeletons, their faces painted in fantastical makeup with white and black and glitter. We stopped and stared when two men rode by on their bicycles. Except they didn't look like men or bicycles. The guys were in bright blue body suits with glowing wings, and when they bent over to ride, flashing blue tails poked out of the back of the bikes, making them look like electric dragonflies.

New Orleans could be wild—especially at Halloween—but I loved it. People here were strange and crazy and creative and more open to the supernatural and psychics than other parts of the country. Maybe that's why New Orleans had so many ghosts. Because people here were open to them.

Speaking of ghosts. A trio of jazz musicians appeared on the sidewalk before us. Their dark skin was deathly pale. One had a tuba, another a saxophone, and still another a trumpet with soggy moss dangling from its neck. Their clothes were wet. Water dripped from their hair, flooding in small pools around their feet. I wondered if they'd drowned together and had come back to haunt their favorite place to play. Their music was faint, but upbeat. They jumped and swayed to the rhythm.

"Do you hear that?" I asked. Jason and Hannah were Untouched, but now and then an Untouched might catch a glimpse or snatch a phrase of music from the air—if the ghost energy was strong enough. That's how my dad had seen my mom after I'd helped the Wilkeses cross over. Mom's love had been so strong, her desire to say goodbye so intense, he'd been able to see her. I swallowed back the threat of pain, and focused on the beautiful, haunting music.

Hannah shook her head. "I don't hear anything." She set her case down and put her hands on the latches. "Do I need my EVP recorder?"

Jason unlatched the case with the *specula spiritis*.

I shook my head. "No. Don't worry about it. They're not dangerous. They're musicians," I said, as we walked past. "I don't even think they know we're here." As I said that, the man playing the trumpet opened his eyes and looked straight at me. A ripple of goose bumps shot over my skin as if the air had just dropped twenty degrees, even though there was only a faint nip of autumn in the air. But he just smiled, gave me a nod of his head to let me know he knew perfectly well I was there, then closed his eyes and kept on playing. Ghosts like that weren't part of the Problem.

True, they'd probably be better off crossing over to wherever we go when we die, but they were happy playing their music and they weren't wreaking havoc on the living or popping up trying to kill cardiac patients. Now those malevolent and mischievous ghosts were the ones we mostly had to deal with. It was all we had time for since less than three percent of the entire population was psychic. Class C Psychics were like poorly tuned radios. They could occasionally see and hear ghosts, but couldn't predict when that would happen. Class C Psychics usually worked as administrative staff for Town Psychics' Office or OPI offices. Aunt Elena was a weak Class C Psychic, but had wanted to do more than sit behind a desk. So, she'd opened her own paranormal investigator business to combine her abilities with technology to help fight the Problem.

I scooted past the ghostly gaggle of musicians and led the way to the burnt-out café. I could see the entrance from here. "This is it," I said, stopping just shy of the front door.

"It's dark in there." Jason fidgeted with the latch on the ghost goggle case.

"We're definitely going to need some light." Hannah set down her case, clicked it open, and pulled out a massive flashlight.

That's when I heard it again. A little giggle. The same giggle I'd heard this morning. My heart raced into my throat and my eyes flew to the blackened café door, which hung open. There, standing in the doorway, was a small girl. Her white nightgown was scorched in places, and long patches along her right arm and the right side of her face were blackened from fire. She must've been about five or six when she died. She looked a little sad and very afraid.

Slowly she raised a hand and beckoned me forward. She said only two words: "Help me." And then she disappeared into the blackened husk of the restaurant.

I dashed after the little ghost girl. I couldn't lose her. I couldn't let her stay trapped in this fiery pit.

Chapter Four

Not waiting to put my headlamp on before chasing after a ghost into a burnt-out building at night was a bad idea. It was pitch-black inside. Darker than night. The air was filled with stale, smoky air and mildew born of stagnant water. But the ghost girl seemed skittish, and I didn't want to lose my chance.

I immediately opened up my psychic senses. That was getting easier to do now. I could see and hear ghosts easily when they wanted me to, but now I was getting good at feeling them out, too. I couldn't see her anywhere, but then again it was pitch-black. "Hello? Are you there?" I called out, my voice echoing off the charred walls.

Suddenly the room filled with blue light. I jerked my head toward the brilliant glow. Jason was standing beside me. Ghost goggles on with the slit open wide to filter out the blue light, we could see for five or six feet around us. It wasn't so bright that I had to squint like when Hannah blasted me with a flashlight. It was actually kinda perfect.

"Very cool, J." I grinned at him. "Do you see anything?" With the *specula spiritis*, Jason could see outlines of ghosts.

Beep. Beep. Beep. Beep. Beep.

Hannah came up on my left side, EMF detector in hand. "This is weird," she said, scanning the meter around the room as the EMF detector beeped erratically. "The readings are unusual. There's something here, but it's like it's spread out. It's not like there's one spot with high energy, like when we have a spirit. Do either of you see anything?"

Jason scanned the room like a mad scientist with glowing glasses, then shook his head. "Nothing."

"What about you, Alex?" Hannah asked as the EMF detector beeped again.

I unfurled my senses further, trying to pin down what I was feeling. "You're right. There's something here. It feels different, but I don't know what."

"Well, why did you run in here like that without being prepared?" It sounded more like an accusation than a question, but I wasn't about to get into an argument about it with Hannah. She was super good at preparation. I was better at action.

"Because I saw her." I pointed toward the set of double swinging doors that led to the kitchen where the little ghost girl had just reappeared.

Jason stayed plastered to his spot, but his gaze remained fixed on the ghost. "I—I can see her. It's—it's a little girl."

Hannah held the EMF detector toward the spot we were looking and the readings blinked off the charts. "Well, that's what those things are supposed to do, right? Help you see ghosts." She stomped her foot. "I don't see why you and Madame Monique won't make me a pair," she mumbled, then switched on her new EVP recorder.

"We're still in the trial phase," Jason said without turning away from the girl. "Once they're fully developed, I'll see about making you some."

The little girl motioned me forward with a curl of two translucent fingers. "Um, can we discuss the ghost goggles later, please?" My heart sped up a tad, and I swallowed back dread. "She wants to show me something."

I stepped toward her and Hannah's hand shot out to stop me. "Are you sure it's safe, Alex?"

"No," I said, shaking her gently free. "But if we're going to help her cross over, I have to find out what she wants, right?"

Hannah swallowed, then nodded.

"Have your holy water ready. Just in case," I said, sounding way more calm and brave than I felt.

"We've got your back, X." Jason gave me a nervous thumbs-up, and I knew he was really scared because he'd used my old childhood nickname, "X."

Knowing they were behind me ready with holy water and sea salt was comforting, but I still had no idea what I was about to face. I walked forward anyway, and the girl reached out her hand. I didn't want to take it. I really didn't. It was going to be bone-achingly cold. But if it's what I had to do to help her, then I'd do it.

So, I reached out my hand and let her fingers curl around mine.

There was no wave of frigid energy like I usually got when Mrs. Wilson touched me. No cool, tingly feeling like I got with Onyx. No ice-bath chill like with the malevolent spirits I'd encountered. Instead, my world went from a muggy October chill to an all-consuming heat.

I opened my eyes, struggling to see, but I was surrounded in fire and smoke. Voices cried out. Men and women screamed in the distance. Orangish-red flames licked up the walls around me. I heard a small girl's voice cry out. My voice. It was as if somehow I'd become the little girl and I was seeing what she had seen.

"Mama! Papa! Mama!" I coughed and couldn't stop. It was getting harder and harder to breathe. And it was hot. So hot. Brutally hot. Sweat plastered my stringy brown hair to my forehead, and my nightgown clung to my legs, making it hard to move.

"Alice!" I heard a woman's voice. Frantic. Terrified. It was the girl's mama. My mama.

"Get out, Emma. Take as much of the silver with you as you can. I'll get Alice," a man with a heavy French accent said. Actually, it wasn't just a French accent. He was speaking French, but somehow I understood it. And the man. He was my papa.

"Papa," I screamed. I was beneath a table. I could see that now. Hiding from the smoke and flames and screams.

Papa's legs rushed past as he gathered our most expensive possessions. Arms full with candlesticks and fabric, Papa bent down and peered under the heavy oak table where I was hiding. "Come, Alice."

I held my arms out to him, tears streaming down my face. I couldn't go out there into the smoky room. Into the fire. Not on my own. It was too scary. "Carry me, Papa. Carry me!"

"I cannot." He hefted his overloaded arms before me, his voice stern. "Come, now!"

"No!" I crossed my arms over my chest and scooted back against the wall. I would not run out into the smoke and flames. Not without Papa to carry me.

Papa let out a frustrated growl. "Do not move! I will be right back for you."

He dashed out the front door, and a beam from the ceiling collapsed in flames. The table above me groaned and thick black smoke choked out the light. I screamed for Papa. I screamed and cried until my throat burned and smoke and heat choked out my breath. I screamed until my world faded into searing blackness.

I coughed, trying to get the nasty smoke out of my lungs, and struggled to sit up. But I was still in the burning building. Only this time I wasn't under the table. I wasn't the little girl anymore. I looked at my pale arms, dark T-shirt, jeans, the scuffed toes of my work boots. I was me again. Alex.

Flames and smoke were all around me, but they didn't burn. The air felt clear, and it was easy to breathe. It was like I was living in a movie from the past. I could see and hear everything going on around me, but I couldn't feel it. I was standing where the little girl's father had been standing. Alice. Her name was Alice.

The room was like a matchbox, the wooden furniture feeding the flames. In front of me was a large oak table. It sagged under the weight of the heavy ceiling beam, coated with flames. Tendrils of smoke and fire filled the room, but I was safe. This had happened, but in the past. Somehow Alice was showing me the past. I crouched down like her papa had done and peered under the table.

Alice was there. Not the living, crying, screaming Alice. The dead one. Her nightgown and face and arms were charred black and I could see through her even though she was almost solid. She watched me nervously, a bit like a frightened cat.

"Alice?" I asked, trying to smile at her even though fiery pieces of building rained down around us. "Why don't you come with me? I can help you find your parents." I hoped. If I could get her to cross over, then I was sure she would see her parents again. By the furniture and clothing, I was sure they'd been dead for a long time.

"Uh-uh." She shook her head and scooted away from me, just like she'd done to get away from her father in the fire.

"Why not?" I asked, crouching lower. Mom had told me it was best to get down low when talking to kids so you were at their eye level. That way you'd seem smaller and less intimidating. Thinking of Mom made my heart ache. "You know, I lost my mom, too."

She looked up at me with big, soulful eyes. It was as if she were about to speak, then terror consumed her and she fell backward against the wall, her body shaking.

"What's wrong?" I asked, wondering if I'd be let out of this hellish ghost vision if she didn't come with me.

She pointed to a spot just over my shoulder. "Be— because. He won't let me."

As I turned to see who was behind me, a huge, charred man with bulging muscles and crazy-looking, bloodshot eyes stomped over to me, circled my neck in his massive, calloused hands, and squeezed.

I kicked and hit and bit at the thing that was holding me. It felt as though he was made of darkness. His icy hands turned from burning cold to a blazing heat in seconds, and he threw me back into the raging fire. Smoke filled my lungs, and I kicked again, struggling to reach into my pocket for the holy water.

My fingers touched the glass rim, but my vision dimmed. I gasped, then coughed out another breath from my smoke-filled lungs. If I didn't get this monster away from me soon, I would black out. If I blacked out, I would die.

I yanked the holy water free from my pocket, and in a blind moment of habit I popped the lid. Then, just as I prepared to toss the contents on the malevolent spirit, a burning smack hit my hand and the water went flying.

I was dead.

Chapter Five

The next thing I knew, I was sitting up and dripping wet. I was in the burnt-out shell of the café, the lingering scent of smoke and mold and beignets twisting in the air. I coughed and gasped in breaths full of clean air. I wasn't dead. And the fiery man with bloodshot eyes was nowhere to be seen.

Jason and Hannah were there. They knelt on either side of me, holding my shoulders. Each had an empty bottle of holy water in their hands. No wonder I was soaked. They must've doused me with it.

Jason's eyes were bug-out wide, the ghost glasses shoved up on his forehead. "Are you okay?"

Even Hannah looked weirded out. "You were shaking and coughing and kicking...and your body started smoking. Like, literally. There was smoke coming off your clothes. Then we threw the holy water on you and the smoke vanished. Poof. Gone. And you sat up gasping for air."

"Yeah. All that. So, what just happened, X?" Jason slid the *specula spiritis* back over his eyes and scanned the room, the blue lights from the goggles ghostly against the burnt-out remains.

"Um..." I coughed one last time to clear the phantom smoke from my lungs and looked all over the restaurant just to make sure there were no ghosts nearby ready to plunge me back into the smoky pit of memories. "I—I'm not sure exactly. I saw the little girl. Then I was back in the past. It was like I was living what happened. And there was this mean man. Worse than Mr. Wilkes." Fear crawled over me like spiders, making goose bumps prickle along my skin when I thought of his bloodshot eyes and charred skin. I shook my head clear of the image and stood on quivering legs. "We can't stay here."

"But it's our job. Our case." Hannah's voice held the hint of panic. "I may have caught an EVP. I could catch more. We can't just leave."

"Trust me," I said. "We have to. There's something here we're not prepared to deal with. We need Frank and Elena's help." There was no way I was going to make the same mistakes I'd made at Lafitte's Bar. No way was I going to risk my friends' lives again. I hauled my work bag up over my shoulder and led them out the front door. "We need to do research first. Until we know what we're up against, I'm not putting anyone in danger."

Hannah led the way down the well-worn brick and paved streets of the French Quarter to Elena's shop, cutting across Jackson Square so we'd arrive more quickly. When I'd asked why we were going there, she'd said nothing.

If I hadn't been annoyed with her for not trusting that I could handle the job, I would have laughed. It reminded me of when I'd first met Hannah. Back when I thought she was a Pretender, someone who was pretending to be psychic, but wasn't. Back when I thought I was still Untouched. I remembered the first time I'd come to Elena's shop. It was not long after my accident and Dad didn't want me home alone because he was worried I thought I was seeing ghosts. At least now he knew I could see ghosts, and while he wasn't okay with it, he accepted it. Yep. A lot had changed for me since last summer, and Elena's shop, too, by the looks of it. We stopped just outside her store, an unusually cool autumn breeze tickling my cheeks and twisting Hannah's dark brown hair.

Through the glass storefront, glittering with protective sigils and spooky-cute Halloween decorations of bats and pumpkins, I could see Elena bent over some books. Elena was building quite a library for herself, and her store was being visited more and more often by psychics. I was sure that Frank had something to do with that.

"So, uh, why are we at Elena's instead of Frank's?" Jason asked, glancing up at the wooden sign that announced Elena's shop.

Hannah sighed and pushed her thick-rimmed glasses up her nose. "I don't like that we had to leave the job. And I'm sorry if I was annoyed with you, Alex," she said. "But Aunt Elena and I were talking. There is a learning curve to all of this—for all of us. So, if Alex is right and we need to do more research first, I thought we might have a look at some of Elena's books. Besides, I know Frank is on the hospital job and Aunt Elena has to be here today to tend the shop."

"Makes sense to me." I gave her a half-smile. Typical, practical Hannah. She was annoying sometimes, but I loved her.

She returned my smile with her own, then opened the door.

Tinging-a-tring. The newly hung door chime tinkled as we entered.

Toward the back right of the store, before the counter, was a large round table where Elena met with clients or discussed cases with Frank. In the room behind the counter was where Elena studied her findings on specially warded computers where she could analyze the data from her EVP recorder and electromagnetic field detector. It's also where she kept her personal supplies for when she went on cases with Frank.

Elena looked up from her notes as soon as we walked in.

"Yes. We're okay. But why are you here? I thought you went to the hospital with Frank?" Hannah set her gunmetal gray paranormal investigator kit on the table and took a seat.

"We were at the hospital, but Gallows turned up and was making it difficult for me to work the case. Besides, I was running low on supplies." Elena shrugged. "So, I came back here to work on my notes."

Hannah nodded. "I'm sorry Gallows got in the way."

"Me, too. Thankfully, he's usually too busy to be much of a bother." She patted Hannah on the hand. "So, what happened at the café?"

"Something weird happened to Alex, and we came back to do some research before going back. I also want to run my data through your computer to see if I caught anything." Hannah patted her PI and motioned toward Elena's computers.

Elena's X-ray eyes swung to me. "Alex?" She stood, walked over to where I was taking stock of the PI gear, and touched my forehead with a cool hand. "Are you okay?"

"Fine. I'm fine," I said, even though I could still taste the hint of smoke on my lips.

"Tell me what happened." Elena led us back to the table, set out bottles of water for everyone, and gave us each a bag of chips.

Hannah ignored the snack and immediately went to investigate what she'd captured on her equipment, but Jason plopped down, ripped open his bag, and shoveled a couple chips immediately into his mouth.

I pushed my bag of chips toward him and sat. The last thing I felt like doing right now was eating. Then, I told Elena everything that had happened from the first time I caught a glimpse of the girl, Alice, to my weird trip to the past. About the girl. About their old-fashioned clothes. About how they spoke French, but I still understood them. And about the fire and the terrible presence. "I think he's keeping her trapped there somehow, but I'm not really sure."

Elena's brows were knitted, and she had a worried expression I didn't see too often. "Has that ever happened to you before?"

"What? Going back in time, understanding a language I don't speak, and reliving the past?" I asked, shaking my head no.

"But you didn't go back in time. You were on the floor right in front of me and Jason, moaning and twitching," Hannah said to me from over her shoulder where she was downloading EVP files to one of Elena's computers. Then she turned to Elena. "But there was smoke coming off his clothes and he was coughing and gasping for air as if he were in a fire." Hannah sounded as if she were trying to solve a mental puzzle, but I frowned at her description of me.

Jason shrugged. "You did twitch and moan, X. Now that I think about it, you looked kinda funny." His voice was serious, but he couldn't keep the grin off his face.

I must've looked ridiculous. I crumpled up a piece of paper and tossed it across the table at him.

"Well, it's true. It was like you were doing some sort of weird floor dance," Hannah said with a grin, but quickly got serious again. "It was like the holy water we dumped on you put the fire out. That's when you woke up... I may have caught something. Let me listen." She pulled on a set of headphones and turned back to the monitor.

"It may be true, but nothing about it is funny." Frank's deep voice rumbled from the entrance of the store.

My body sagged with relief. All the worry and tension I'd been holding since being hurled back in time to see Alice's last moments alive had suddenly left me. Frank was here, and I was safe. Now we could figure out what was going on.

"I thought you were going to stay at the hospital." Elena's eyebrows rose in surprise at Frank's unexpected appearance.

"I was, but there's been another flare-up. It seems like we're getting a new ghost almost every time someone dies. Something's holding them there. OPI's got a shipment of salt coming in tomorrow, but I'm out of salt at home, so I thought I'd swing by here to get some more."

"How long were you standing there?" Elena asked, while pulling a few massive sacks of salt from the storeroom.

"Long enough to hear what Alex experienced." Frank took a seat and rubbed the scruff on his chin in a world-weary way. "I'm going to see if the feds can call in a few OPI officers from another fire case. You need a mentor, and right now they've got me so busy it's as if I never retired."

"They still don't have you back on the payroll?" Elena asked with a smirk.

My heart clinched in my chest. If Frank officially went back to work for the OPI, then I wouldn't have a teacher. And if I didn't have a teacher, then I'd be sent off to some psychic boarding school that could deal with a too-old newbie psychic—either that or I'd be forced to find a new mentor.

Frank raised his eyebrows at her. "My priority is Alex. Period."

I sighed a little too loudly, and Frank looked at me. "I agreed to be your teacher until you're able to become a Certified Psychic. So, you're stuck with me until you're sixteen. Got it?"

I nodded, but if Frank was worried enough about whatever happened to me to tell OPI to take a backseat, then I must really be in trouble. The wave of relief I'd felt with him here suddenly seemed to disappear. "So, what was that? What happened to me when I saw what the ghost saw and felt what she felt?" I asked, feeling like I'd swallowed an ostrich egg. "She definitely didn't look modern." I gulped. "And we know no kids died in the Quarter fires last week. So, who is she?"

Frank studied me like he did the first time we met, and I felt as if he could see straight through me. Then he shook his head, leaned back, and stared at the ceiling.

"Here." Elena shoved a bottle of water at him. "Have a drink."

Frank unscrewed the plastic cap and took a long gulp. "I'm not sure who she is, but that's not what's important right now. What's important is you. If you experienced what I think you did, then you have a very powerful, very rare gift. There are only three psychics in recorded history—since the Problem started anyway—that have ever reported actually living through what a spirit experienced at his or her death. It's called the Sight. And it would mean you're a Seer."

Great. Just great. Along with being a freakishly old baby psychic, I might have an extra rare power: I might now be able to relive people's deaths. My stomach took a plunge to my toes. Fan-freaking-tastic!

Frank put a comforting hand on my forearm, pulling me from my worry. "We have to see if it happens again before we can confirm anything. If it does, then we'll work with it, Alex. I know what you saw must've been scary. Seeing someone die is upsetting."

Boy, was he right. And feeling it had been even worse. I thought of the little girl, Alice. She'd been so terrified. Her fear had burned into my bones. I'd smelled the smoke. Felt the heat. Fire and fear twisted together in a terrible dance that led the girl to her death.

"If you do have this power, then we'll help you use it to your advantage." Frank's voice echoed in my ears, even though my mind was still trapped in the smoky, fire-filled room with Alice.

Elena wrapped her arms around me, squeezing warmth and life back into me. "If you know how they lived and died, then you'll be able to help even the toughest spirits cross over."

"Well, the first thing we need to do before plunging Alex back into some weird, fiery memory is find out what happened there. You were right, Alex." Hannah looked at me, and her acknowledgment that I'd made the right decision to leave the job brought me straight back to reality. "I caught an EVP, Alex. A good one. But I don't know what it means."

"Let's hear it." Elena walked over to the computer and pressed a button. Static. Then our voices. Then a distorted male voice, but close. It was as if the ghost had been standing beside Hannah. The voice said, "*Brûlez...*" then more static. The voice continued, but it was garbled.

Hannah groaned. "It's good, but I didn't capture enough of it. I wish I could have seen what he looked like."

"That's okay. It sounds like a man's voice. French?" Elena rubbed her chin and glanced at Frank.

"I think so. That may be the dark presence you felt, Alex," Frank said. "Did you get a little girl's voice at all?"

Hannah shook her head, but looked determined. "Not yet."

"Okay. Well, let's see if we can find out what *brûlez* means." Elena sat beside Hannah and pulled up a translation program and typed a word into her computer.

"Burn." Hannah read the word, her voice quavering. "It means burn."

Elena and Frank looked at each other, worry clear on their faces.

"You were right, Alex," Hannah said with a gulp. "It's good we left. Before any of us go back there, we need to find out what happened in that café. Like you said, we know that no kids died in the café fire, only adults. So the girl you saw must've died in another fire."

"And by the sound of it, a fire from a long time ago," Elena said. "And if that man was part of her memory or whatever you saw, he might have died in the same fire..." She stood up and skimmed her bookcases. "I don't have many history books here. My collection is focused on the history of paranormal investigation, modern PI methods and equipment advances, and case studies on how PIs and psychics can work together."

"I have a lot on local history," Frank said. "Especially when it concerns crime, accidents, and deaths. Go have a look in the apartment. See what you can find about fires. I know there were huge fires in the Quarter in 1788 and 1794 when the city was made mostly of wood. But first, we need to get some sleep. All of us." Frank took out his sigil-inscribed brass pocket watch. He claimed it was better than my Spellguard or Hannah's WardWing because it had no electronics; he had to wind it up manually. "It's nearly eleven o'clock. We can begin working on this in the morning. When we're fresh."

I wasn't convinced I'd sleep very well all night after reliving a brutal fire from the past, being strangled by a terrifying ghost, and nearly suffocated with smoke, but I *was* tired. "Okay. Fine. Sleep. Then we'll research first thing tomorrow. But whatever we find, I already *know* there's the spirit of a little girl trapped in there with some bad guys saying 'burn.' So, no matter what, we have to help her."

CHAPTER SIX

Someone was staring at me, the weight of their eyes pressing me down.

"Mrs. Wilson?" I grumbled without opening my eyes.

Suddenly, Onyx pounced on my chest, pushing a gush of air from my lungs.

Merow.

I groaned, opened my eyes, patted his chilly head, and looked at my windup alarm clock. It was a few minutes past ten o'clock in the morning.

Onyx leapt off me and disappeared through my bedroom wall as if to say "time to get up and get a move on!"

I stumbled out of bed and called Jason from the kitchen phone—the only phone in the apartment. Frank insisted we use an antique willow wood wall phone that sounded like a clanging streetcar when it rang. Apparently, it was the safest phone Frank could find because of the type of wood and the fact the wires were encased in iron. It was made a couple decades after the Problem started, and whoever had made it had gone crazy with the protective seals they'd wood-burned into it, which Frank loved. Of course Frank had redone the iron ward paint himself.

"Hannah's already called me three times!" Jason moaned in a voice that said he was still in bed and had no intention of getting up early on a Saturday morning. "I just want to go back to sleep."

"Still asleep, isn't he?" Shaggy brows quirked, Frank gave me an amused expression and stuffed his mouth with a fluffy pancake.

"What if pancakes are involved?" I watched Mrs. Wilson's huge, translucent rump wiggle as she beat another round of pancake batter. The smell of flapjacks and warm maple syrup Mrs. Wilson was cooking up was already making my mouth water. She used my mom's recipe, and her pancakes were just like Mom's. My heart gave a twisted pinch. Boy, did I miss Mom. Dad was super busy with work, but I saw him some weekends. It had been weeks now since I'd seen him. When I did, it was okay, but weird. Things just weren't the same at home without Mom there. It was like home wasn't home anymore. I missed Mom a lot. Dr. Midgley, the psychiatrist I'd been seeing since the accident, said the first year after losing someone was the hardest. I hoped he was right.

"Tell that boy to get himself on over here. I'll make extra for him. With chocolate chips." Mrs. Wilson might be a ghost, but she had supersonic hearing. I could *never* have a private conversation when she was around. It seemed like she could hear me from anywhere in the apartment.

"Mrs. Wilson's making you extra, J. With chocolate chips."

"I'm getting dressed now." I heard the shuffle of clothes just before he hung up the phone.

"He's on his way," I told Mrs. Wilson, helping myself to a nice sticky finger coated in maple syrup.

She playfully swatted my hand away with a dripping spoon of pancake batter. "Save it for the hotcakes! Frank already invited Hannah and that auntie of yours. I'm ready to pass a good time and have a big ol' family breakfast," she smiled and began humming some old tune I didn't recognize.

"While you're waiting for reinforcements, why don't you start going through the books in the office. See if you can find something to get you started on the café research." Frank took a big sip of coffee and set his cup down with a thud on the breakfast table.

"Aren't you coming with us today?" My shoulders suddenly got tight, and I jammed my hands in my pockets. I didn't know what we were dealing with, and while I didn't want to admit it, I was afraid. Maybe that was normal for kids who weren't fully Certified Apprentice Psychics.

"Yes, we're coming. I've made arrangements for someone else to cover for us at the hospital. While you kids are doing the initial research, Elena and I just need to finish up some paperwork on the last hospital ghost we helped with. The feds like everything in writing. So, we need to get this report turned in. They're very impressed with her so far. Her equipment, data, and analysis have given external confirmation of what the psychics are seeing, and the higher-ups like that." He took another long sip. "Most of 'em are retired field officers. So, if they can't be there to see and hear what happened, they have to rely on our reports. With some of Elena's EVPs they can actually get audio confirmation right in their cozy D.C. offices of what the field officers have heard."

"And they like that?"

"Oh, they like that a lot. It's a good way to ensure that field officers aren't fabricating details. It's something I don't think they considered until Elena got involved." Frank finished off his coffee with a final swig.

It made sense, but it was kind of weird that they'd been so anti-PI before now. I mean the equipment was getting better, but from what I'd read, the psychics trusted the Untouched about as much as the Untouched wanted to trust us. Maybe if we could all start relying on each other more, that trust would improve. "Makes sense," I said with a nod. "I'll go see what I can find before they get here."

Frank's office had an entire wall of books. There were paperbacks and hardcovers, even many leather-bound tomes with gold and silver titles and symbols. I'd read some of his books since I'd moved in last month, but mostly I'd only skimmed. There were books on wards, protection sigils, the history of occult studies, spirits, angels, demons, and a variety of supernatural entities. And, of course, there was history. At least there were books on the city's darker side of history.

I skimmed my finger along the section of history books Frank had organized.

Merow.

Onyx leapt up onto the bookshelf so he was eye level with me and headbutted my hand as an invitation to give him a rub.

"Hi Onyx." I tickled the cool fur behind his ears, and I ran my hand down his back and along his tail. He arched up like a Halloween cat. "Can you help me find a book on New Orleans' fires? Frank said there were two big fires, 1788 and 1794."

Onyx's green eyes fixed on mine for a moment, then with another meow, he leapt up a shelf and started rubbing and purring against a tattered cloth volume with gold lettering.

I grabbed the book Onyx was rubbing. *Hidden History: New Orleans in the Sixteenth to Eighteenth Centuries.* Hmm. How did Onyx know how to find books? He was like my own personal library cat. "Two hundred years is a lot of history to cover," I said. "Couldn't you have gotten me something a little more specific?"

Merow. He licked his paw and casually rubbed it over his ear, as if to say, *I've done what you asked and found the book. Now do the rest yourself.*

I laughed and shook my head. Never in a trillion years would I have expected to have a pet ghost cat who could locate books. It was so weird. But very cool. "Okay, well, you can at least sit with me while I read."

I curled up in the overstuffed leather chair by the fireplace so I could peer out the window toward Royal Street. It was a good place to think. I gazed through the myriad of symbols etched in the glass and spied an angelic-looking specter peering in at me.

She must have been around seventeen or eighteen. She gave me a pretty smile.

I avoided direct eye contact so I didn't risk having her try to communicate with me and somehow get sucked back into the past to see how she died; I had enough to deal with right now without that. Still, she looked sweet, so I smiled back.

That's when her hair pillowed up around her in a great billowy puff of windy smoke and the flesh crackled from her cheeks. Her smile turned into a feral, black-lipped snarl. She snapped her lips together and disappeared in a puff of flames.

I guess that's what I deserved for smiling back at some pretty dead girl. I shook my head at myself. I didn't need any more encouragement to stop gazing and start reading. There was definitely something going on here with fire and ghosts in the city. I flipped open the book and skimmed the table of contents, mindlessly scratching my nearly healed forearms. As soon as I was a full apprentice and had completed my basic psychic studies,

I'd get my Psychic Apprentice card. Then I'd feel like I'd actually accomplished something. I stopped scratching when my eyes reached chapter 4: "The Great New Orleans Fire of 1788." Wow. A whole chapter on a big fire. Maybe this was the one I needed.

I glanced down at Onyx, who was curled up on my lap pretending to sleep. At least I thought he was pretending. As far as I knew, ghosts didn't need sleep. Why would they? I mean, they were dead. I still wondered how it was he'd found this book for me, just like he'd found the one to help me with the Lafitte case. I supposed it didn't matter. I was just lucky to have him. He must've read my thoughts because he gave a giant stretch, embedded his ghost claws into my jeans, and started kneading. Right. A psychic-librarian-ghost cat.

I tickled him behind the ears, flipped open the book to chapter 4, and started to read an account by Governor Esteban Rodriquez Miró.

> On the evening of the 21st of March 1788, at 1:30 o'clock, a fire broke out in the private residence of Don Vicente Jose Nunez, paymaster of the army. (This building was situated at the lower corner of Chartres and Toulouse Streets.)

I was silently glad the old governor had written down those street names. That was going to make it so much easier to find out where the fire started and, hopefully, figure out what was going on. If this was, in fact, the fire Alice had died in.

I kept reading:

Eight hundred and fifty-six buildings were reduced to ashes, including all the business houses and principal mansions of the city. A wind from the south, then blowing with fury, thwarted every effort... The public jail was also destroyed, and we had no time to save the lives of the unfortunate prisoners.

Ugh. That wasn't good. If they hadn't saved the prisoners from the fire and they had all died trapped in jail, then there might be a lot of mean, angry prison ghosts to deal with. Even more reason to get this fire figured out, and fast.

I continued reading about everything that they'd managed to save, about how devastating the fire had been, about the hundreds who had lost their homes and businesses, even family members, to the blaze.

The tears, the heart-breaking sobs and the pallid faces of these wretched people mirrored the dire fatality that had overcome a city, now in ruins, transformed within the space of five hours into an arid and fearful desert. Such was the sad ending of a work of death, the result of seventy years of industry.

I finished Governor Miró's account, then sat there dully studying the old map depicting the area of the New Orleans fire. Eight hundred and fifty-six buildings had burned. Most of what was now the French Quarter had been destroyed. Seventy years of building and work. Gone. In five hours.

It reminded me sorely of how fast my life had changed. The honk of horns. The screech of metal. The crush of breaking glass. Seconds to shred my hip, kill my mom, and devastate my life. I hadn't realized it before, but in a way that accident had destroyed my home, too. Life with Dad would never be the same. Home would never be the same. And that's what had happened to this city in that fire. To my city. To all those poor people. Their homes had been destroyed. And their lives. It's no wonder there were ghosts trapped here from such a horrible, heart-wrenching event.

"But why now?" I asked Onyx, who lay gazing up at me. "The fire was over two hundred years ago. If this was the fire that killed Alice and the other ghosts people are reporting, why are they just appearing now?"

As if in answer to my question, the buzzer rang at the door, and Jason's, Hannah's, and Elena's voices floated up to our second-story home. I was glad they were here, and as soon as we finished breakfast, we were going to find out if the Great Fire was what had caused Alice's death.

"I brought whipped cream!" Jason grinned, then whipped out the can and shot some into his mouth. "Now, where are the pancakes?"

Just over an hour later, our bellies filled with pancakes and Jason's lips and chin still smeared with chocolate chips and maple syrup—a dab of whipped cream stuck to his nose—Hannah, Jason, and I made our way to the New Orleans Historic Library. In what seemed like minutes, the librarian had Jason and me loaded down with maps and copies of old documents, and Hannah had jumped right into the historical record books.

"According to what I just read," Hannah said, emerging from behind a thick book, "the Great Fire of 1788 burned nearly seventy-eight percent of the city. And that's why we don't have French architecture today. Many people still spoke French, but it was under Spanish rule. So, they rebuilt things in the Spanish style."

"Huh. I always thought it was weird there were so many Spanish buildings here when there're so many French names," Jason said. "But that makes sense."

I leaned over Jason to study the map he had out. "The chapter I read at the apartment was an account from the governor at the time. He said that house where the fire started was located here." I pointed to a square on the map at the corner of Chartres and Toulouse Streets.

"Okay. So we need to find out what was located there back then, if that's possible, and what's there today. Maybe that'll give us a clue about why it's being haunted." Hannah adjusted her thick-rimmed glasses on the bridge of her nose and peered at the map in front of us.

"Originally it was the house of the army paymaster... I can't remember his name, but it was a house back then." I shrugged. "I have no idea what's there now."

"Here." Jason laid out the black-and-white photocopy on the table. It was a much newer map than the others we'd seen. Instead of empty blocks of a newly laid-out city with markers for a cemetery, prison, and church, there were notations about popular tourist attractions, freeways, and steamboats. The familiar Ursuline Convent was the only constant I could spy between the maps, even if it was a museum now. "It's just a copy of a tourist map, but the librarian said we can mark on it if we need to."

Hannah pulled a highlighter from her school bag. "Great!"

"What're you doing?" Jason asked, an edge of fright in his voice, as if we were going to have to do a major school project.

Grinning, Hannah pulled the copy of the tourist map toward her. "I'm going to highlight the area that the fire affected over the modern city. That way we can tell what's where today. If we just look at these old maps, I don't think we'll get very far."

"Good idea." Even though Hannah was an average student, I knew she was really smart. She just got bored with the *usual* homework. But give her something paranormal and she was all over it. If there was ever a paranormal investigator school started, she'd be the first one to sign up.

Jason and I read off street names from the old map of where the fire started and how many blocks it extended in every direction. Hannah first marked the boundaries of the fire on the photocopy of the modern map, then we all double-checked the cross streets to be sure we had the right area marked. Once we were sure it was correct, Hannah swished the highlighter back and forth until there was a blazing yellow trapezoid right in the middle of the French Quarter.

"There." Hannah snapped the lid back on the highlighter with a satisfying click. "Now we can see exactly what we're dealing with."

I traced my finger along the blocks of yellow that had been taken out by the blaze, then along the roads to find the corner of Chartres and Toulouse Streets. "The fire started here," I said, marking it with a pen. "Only one block from the Cabildo, and whatever was there at the time burned in 1788."

"The café is right next door to the Cabildo. Just down from where the original fire started. Maybe it was housing back then." Hannah chewed on the tip of the highlighter before scrounging around the table for another map. "I'm still not sure how this all fits together."

"I remember going on a field trip to the Cabildo in third grade when we were studying New Orleans history, but I don't remember learning anything about this fire," Jason said. "That fire took out most of the French Quarter. A lot of people must've died."

"Yeah. It sounded like it was really awful when I read about it. But I couldn't find anything about how many died. Except that they weren't able to save the prisoners." Saying it out loud made the whole situation seem even worse—IF this was the fire that had caused Alice and that terrible man to die.

Hannah gasped. "They left the prisoners to burn to death?"

"The governor seemed sorry about it in his letter. It sounds like the fire burned really fast because of the wood and wind. They just didn't have time. In five hours most of the city was destroyed."

"Pretty amazing how fast a fire could destroy almost an entire city," Jason said.

Just like it only took seconds for an accident to destroy my life.

Jason ran his hands through his super-short hair. "Do you think that whatever was choking you could have been one of the prisoners?"

I shrugged. It was possible. But until I spoke to the ghosts to figure out when they'd died, I couldn't know for sure.

Hannah, peering from atop another map, rejoined the conversation. "Look what I found..." She turned the old map she'd been studying around so we could see it. "The Cabildo *is* the location of the old prison."

A sick feeling writhed its way into the pit of my stomach, making me want to puke. The café was next to the Cabildo. If the Cabildo was the location of the old prison, then it was possible that any trapped spirits could move into the café. Especially if any of the buildings' boundaries had changed when they'd been rebuilt. Mean old murderous Mr. Wilkes had been bad enough, but trying to cross over a bunch of ticked-off, fiery, dead inmates? Ugh. I didn't know if I was up for this. I wasn't even a Certified Apprentice Psychic yet. And I sure didn't want to put Jason and Hannah in danger if I didn't have to. As if answering my thoughts, Hannah chimed in.

"Well, there's only one way to find out if we're dealing with victims from the 1788 fire." Hannah rolled up our highlighter-marked map and tucked it into the new messenger bag she was using for our casework.

"And how's that?" Jason's voice trembled, like he really didn't want to hear what she was going to say. But I knew the words before they even left her lips.

"We go back to the café to investigate, and Alex can have another chat with the ghosts to find out when they died."

CHAPTER SEVEN

We hurried back to the apartment to tell Elena and Frank what we'd found and to get our gear so we could start our work at the café while it was still light outside.

As soon as we walked in the door to the apartment, I knew there was trouble. Mrs. Wilson was wringing her hands. Elena was packing up her PI kit. And Frank looked like he'd swallowed a brick. "There've been two more fires within three blocks of the café. All since last night."

"What?" Hannah rushed in and joined Elena in hurriedly packing up the remaining pieces of PI equipment that had been out for testing.

"Thankfully, no one died. Four people are in the hospital with minor burns and smoke-inhalation injuries, but there are reports of what Frank and I believe is supernatural activity at the sites of the fires." Elena looked at Hannah. "Make sure you bring your new EVP recorder. I'm hoping you can catch more this time."

"So you think something paranormal is causing them?" I asked, grabbing my psychic investigator satchel.

"I'm not sure yet, but it seems likely. What'd you find at the library?"

While we packed up to go, Jason, Hannah, and I told Elena and Frank everything we'd learned. "So, Alex needs to find out if Alice died in 1788. If she did, then that might give us a clue as to what's going on and who's haunting the place," said Hannah.

"True. But it doesn't answer the question of why they're appearing now. And why all the new fires?" I said, not liking the way this cluster of cases was shaping up.

"We definitely need to find out why these fires are happening and if they're related, and what's stirring up these ghosts." Frank cinched his bag over his shoulder, and Elena grabbed her PI kit. "We need psychics and paranormal investigators at both locations to get as much information as we can. Elena and Jason, you go with Alex. Hannah, you come with me—"

"But!" Hannah protested. "We're a team. You can't split us up!"

Frank opened his mouth, but Elena stopped him. "She's right, Frank. I know it's dangerous. But they need to learn to work together. And there's no evidence it's an active site; what Alex is picking up is from the past. Besides, we'll be just around the corner. If they need help, one of them can run and get us."

Aunt Elena might not think it was an active site, but that man's hands around my throat sure felt active to me—even if I was seeing him in some sort of warped death memory. Team or not, I wasn't so sure I wanted to go back without Frank.

His serious eyes traveled over each of us, and I could see Frank weighing Elena's words. "You're almost a full apprentice, Alex...and Elena is right. You do need to learn to work together." He let out a deep sigh. "So, Elena and I will go to the site of the new fire and see what we find. As she said, we'll be just around the corner, and you, Jason, or Hannah can get us if we're needed. I don't want anyone getting hurt, understand?"

My mouth went dry. I wanted to tell him I wasn't ready, but then Hannah threw her arms around Frank's neck and gave him a hug that nearly knocked him off his feet. "Oh, thank you! Thank you for trusting us. We won't let you down."

Now how could I tell him I wasn't ready? Besides, Hannah was right. Frank letting us go to investigate the café again on our own was a sign that he *did* trust us. And I knew that trust was hard earned.

"While we're there, Alex, you, Jason, and Hannah set up at the café. Hannah, see if you can get any EVP recordings or EMF fluctuations that coincide with what Alex sees or hears. Jason, take your *specula spiritis* so you can see what's going on. But before any of us goes anywhere, we're making a visit to Madame Monique for fire charms."

Fire charms? I'd never heard of a fire charm. Then again, there were a whole lot of supernatural things I never knew were real a few months ago either.

We walked past the blazing jack-o'-lanterns Madame Monique had in her windows, on the counter, and on every available shelf in the shop. Their faces were scary and friendly, but they made the place feel cozy for Halloween.

"They will help keep the evil spirits away on All Hallows' Eve and on the Day of the Dead." Madame Monique gave us her warm, toothy smile. "The grinning jacks welcome the friendly spirits, and my wards and herbs will encourage them to cross over. The scary faces will keep the evil ones away. Those are the ones you deal with, Monsieur Frank, no? The evil ones?"

Frank raised an eyebrow, but nodded. "Mostly. Yes."

"*Merci*." Madame Monique bobbed her head at us with thanks. "And for each of you I have a fire charm to help in your endeavors."

"How'd she know we needed fire charms?" Hannah whispered, eyes wide.

Jason sucked in a laugh. "Frank probably called her. She's not psychic, Hannah." He grinned and led the way to the counter like he lived there.

"You've only spent a few weekends with her so far. How would you know if she's psychic or not?"

Jason shook his head. "Trust me. She's not psychic."

"Well, I am psychic and I can't read minds or see the future," I said.

"That's true. Everyone's gifts are different," Hannah said thoughtfully.

"Exactly," Jason grinned. "And telling the future isn't one of hers. She's great with herbs and inventions; just like me. Alex is psychic, and you and Elena have the paranormal investigations nailed. We're a great team."

"That we are." Madame Monique's soothing voice was like a warm blanket on a cold night—despite her calling us children.

Madame Monique placed five silver charm bracelets on the counter. One loop of each bracelet held a disc-like charm engraved with something like a Celtic wave. "Silver and iron, just like you requested, Frank," she continued. "The amulets have ancient druid seals that should dampen any spirits trying to threaten you with fire."

Jason gave Hannah an I-told-you-so smirk about Frank having told Madame Monique what he wanted for charms.

Hannah crossed her arms over her chest and studied the bracelets, pretending she hadn't seen Jason.

After securing the bracelets to each of our wrists herself and saying a Haitian prayer, Madame Monique gave us five bottles of Green Ghost for our bags. "And remember," Madame Monique said as we headed out the door. "They are only good for two days. If you don't drink them before that, *pfft*. No good. Toss them out."

It was the evening before Halloween and a Saturday night. Despite fewer tourists due to the recent outbreak of ghosts and fires in New Orleans, the streets were full with Louisianans and Halloween lovers from everywhere. There were some kids out with their parents, but mostly there were adults. In full costume. Drinking what smelled like alcohol. Costumes and alcohol were common in New Orleans—no matter what time of year—but the Halloween season seemed to make adults think they could act and dress even crazier.

My parents never drank too much of the stuff, but Hannah's mom did. Ever since her dad left, her mom had been too into wine. Hannah never really talked about it much, but Jason and I both knew Elena was really the one raising her now. At least she had Elena. And us, of course.

Hannah stiffened as a drunk woman wearing a sequined dress and butterfly wings stumbled into her.

"Oh, I'm sorry, love." She giggled, spilling some beer from her plastic cup and down the front of her shirt.

The man she was with laughed, and pulled her close. "Let's go get you something else to drink."

Hannah just shook her head as they went arm in arm to a nearby bar. "Adults are so stupid sometimes," she mumbled.

"Do you remember the time our parents got drunk, X? It was New Year's Eve, I think." Jason rolled his eyes. "They acted *weird*."

"Yep," I said, not wanting to make Hannah feel bad that our parents had only been drunk once that we could remember. They'd all had a bit too much to drink that night on account of the holiday and had wandered around the house laughing too loudly and chatting like chipmunks with party hats on. They'd let Jason and me stay up way too late. I think we'd gone to sleep around two o'clock in the morning. Of course, that was then. Now that I was an Apprentice Psychic Investigator in training, late nights were normal.

At least it wasn't late. I glanced at my Spellguard. It was just past six o'clock in the evening. The café spirits, if there were any active ones, wouldn't be at full strength until it was dark out, but I had a feeling it was dark enough that we'd get something. Maybe we'd have this investigation wrapped up by 11 p.m. and get to have a normal Halloween tomorrow.

Then I caught a whiff of ghost fire. I smelled it before I could see it. The damp, acrid stink of smoke and mold got stronger the closer we got until, finally, we stood in front of the carcass of the café.

"Well, here we are again," said Hannah, pulling a small table that had somehow escaped the ravaging flames from the café. She placed it just inside what was left of the café door and put her PI gear on it. Theft could be a problem in New Orleans, but almost nobody would bother a psychic investigation. If they did and got caught, they knew the psychics might not help them if they had ghost trouble. That, and the fact most people still didn't like psychics because we were different and had caused the Problem to begin with, meant most people steered clear of us. It was like they were afraid of us. We were a necessary evil. But I was getting used to that.

"Yeah. Here we are again without Frank or Elena," I sighed, attempting to steel my nerves for whatever nightmarish visions might come if I was a Seer. I'd thought Frank would be here with me this time.

"I'll be okay, X." Jason gave me a brotherly arm squeeze and snugged on his *specula spiritis*. "We've got your back." He grinned and his one visible eye looked like some sort of massive bug.

I laughed and shook my head. "I'm glad, J." I squeezed him back. "Just be sure to have your holy water ready in case you need to douse me again."

"Will do. And I'll have these on." He gestured to his spirit glasses and flicked open the little chambers to turn on the light. "So this time I'll be able to see what's happening."

"Sounds good." I took a deep breath, and glanced over to Hannah, who already had her new EVP recorder turned on, and then flicked her EMF detector to life.

"I can't wait until I have something so I can actually see ghosts... Maybe a pair with a video recorder so I can capture what I see and use it as proof!"

"Hmmm," Jason grunted. "We don't use electronics," he said, as though he'd said it a thousand times.

"I know that. But if you make me a pair, I can modify them myself." She grinned.

"We'll see, but I doubt Madame Monique will want one of her inventions to be compromised with electricity. Anyway, you already have a ton of equipment that you use to prove PIs can help with the Problem." Jason spun his gaze over the back wall, throwing an eerie blue light around the room.

"True," Hannah said, then flicked her EMF detector to life. *Beep. Beep. Beep. Beep. Beep.* It blinked red, then stayed a silent, solid green. "Ready. Hopefully, I'll catch something really good this time." She gave us both a determined nod of the head, and I caught a glimpse of the new fire charm dangling brightly from her wrist.

I felt my own bracelet, cool against my skin, and was glad we at least had more protection going in this time than before. "Okay, then." I let out the huge breath I'd been holding. "Let's go."

We walked through the remains of the doorway into the carcass of the building. Nothing was different from last night except that the air was warmer and the last rays of daylight streamed in through the roof today, which made it much easier to see and a heck of a lot less scary.

The temperature suddenly dropped, making chills snake their way up my arms and down my spine. Jason's and Hannah's breaths came out in white puffs, and the EMF detector beeped erratically.

"Do you see anything, X?" Jason swung his head around from one side of the room to the other.

The air seemed to be sucked out of my chest, and my lungs tightened. I tilted my head to one side, listening. "I don't see anything—yet." My voice came out in a muffled whisper. "Do you?"

He shook his head no, but the temperature in the room just seemed to get even colder.

"I've got the EVP recorder going. Why don't you try to talk to them, Alex?" Hannah held up the EVP recorder so I could see the green light was on.

Right. If I was going to become a fully Certified Apprentice Psychic, then I'd better get used to being brave even when I didn't feel it. I swallowed the terror clogging my throat and called out, "Alice?"

I waited.

Nothing but a tiny drip, drip, drip from some place in the café.

"Alice, are you here?" I called again.

A little giggle echoed not two feet on my right.

I froze, half terrified of being hurled back in time, and half hopeful I could help Alice cross over. Then a small, frigid hand slipped into mine, and pulled me toward the back of the store. Pulled me toward the double swinging doors that led to what used to be the café's kitchen. Toward the place I'd seen Alice die.

Stepping through the doors was like stepping back in time. I could smell smoke, but the room wasn't on fire yet. I looked around the room, trying to pick up any clues about the time period, and wished I'd paid more attention in history class. If this was real, it meant I was a Seer. A freakin' Seer. The walls were wood and there were many thick wooden crossbeams. There were a few solid pieces of wood furniture that looked like things my mom and I had seen when I'd gone with her into an antique store, and there was definitely nothing that looked modern. No televisions or radios or computers. And no wards or sigils that I could see. It must have been a time before the Problem started.

A woman from the past, wearing an off-white gown, raced around the room, placing clothes in a trunk. I was back in the movie again. A movie of the last moments of Alice's life.

A man wearing snug pants with a shirt and vest quickly collected metal candlesticks and coins, carefully placing them in a chest. "Alice. Get your belongings and help your mama," he said, his French words filled with worry and fear.

But Alice wasn't looking at the grown-ups. She wasn't even listening to them. Instead, she was staring at me. She was wearing the same white nightgown I'd seen her in the other night, but she didn't look burnt.

"Is this your home?" I asked, knowing it must've been, but wanting her to talk.

"Uh-huh."

"Do you know what year it is?"

A thunderous thud shook the walls, and her eyes darted toward the noise. The first flickers of orange appeared to be eating away the wood in the walls, and the room suddenly grew intensely hot.

It's not real, I told myself. *Not real. I'm living in the past. Seeing what she saw. I need to stay calm and get her to talk to me.* "Alice," I called out to her, but she was no longer standing in front of me. The room began to fill with rancid smoke. The woman cried out and the man rushed around more urgently, their voices raised in panic.

"Alice?" I spun around the room looking for her. Where had she gone?

My eyes snagged the large table where I'd seen her hiding last night. I got near the table and crouched down. Sure enough, she was there. Hiding. Is this what the poor girl did every single night? Relive the terror of her burning to death in the one place she'd felt safe? Burning to death at home? I shuddered. I had to get through to her.

"Alice," I said, as gently as I could. "I need you to talk to me. There is a way we can make this end. You can find a way out of the fire. Would you like that?"

Her dark brown eyes welled up with tears, and she nodded.

"Okay. Good." I reached out my hand to her. "Then I need you to take my hand. Come out of this room with me and we'll talk." As soon as the words left my lips, the building shuddered and the first blazing timber collapsed from the roof and into the room.

I heard the man and woman scream, but I stayed with Alice. They were just residual energy from Alice's memory. She was real. She was here. "Alice," I said in a voice that was scarily like my dad's when he was mad at me.

She looked at me with frightened eyes.

"I know you're scared, but you need to talk to me. Tell me who that bad man is that we saw last night. Tell me what year it is. I want to help you."

Her eyes grew wide, and her bottom lip trembled. She screamed as she pointed at something behind me. Without even looking, I knew he was there. I could feel the heat and smell the acrid smoke of burning flesh. I heard him mumbling something in French. It was that terrible presence. The spiteful spirit. A malevolent ghost.

If I turned around, he would grab me. Choke me. Try to suffocate me. I had to stay focused for Alice for as long as I could. If things went wrong, Jason and Hannah would pull me back.

"Is he a prisoner, Alice? The bad man, does he look like a prisoner?"

Alice curled into a little ball, trying to disappear into the wall, and nodded.

The scorching heat was right up behind me now, the smell of charred flesh flooding my nostrils. My eyes streamed from the smoke and I choked back a cough. "And the year..." I gasped.

Searing hands gripped my neck from behind, the bony fingers crushing my windpipe. "Alice!" I choked, my vision going black. "The...year? So. I. Can. Help. You."

The last thing I heard before I passed out was Alice's frightened whisper.

"1788."

CHAPTER EIGHT

My lungs seared with smoke and I coughed myself awake from the nightmare that had been Alice's last few moments of life. But had that evil man been there like some lurking specter as her parents rushed to save their belongings? Somehow I didn't think so. I hadn't seen him there when she died. He was only there when I saw Alice as a ghost.

"Alex. Alex. Alex!" The panic in Frank's voice forced my eyes open.

Water sopped my hair and rolled down my cheeks and onto my shirt. Droplets dangled from my eyelashes, and I wiped them away to clear my vision. Frank's concerned eyes were the first thing to come into focus, followed by Elena, Jason, and Hannah, who all huddled around me with empty bottles of holy water in their hands.

I coughed again and sat up.

"Take it easy." Frank helped me lean against the burnt-out wall. The same wall against which Alice had been hiding when she died.

"Frank?" Confusion replaced my terror. Where had Frank come from? I scooted to the middle of the room, away from her place of death, suddenly cold and shivering after all the smoke and heat.

"It's okay, Alex." Frank was beside me again, a fatherly arm wrapped around me. "Hannah came and got us. We're here. All of us. It's okay."

"Did you see Alice? What did she say? Was anyone else there?" Hannah's words came out in a stream of excitement. "My EVP recorder picked something up, but I can't tell what it is yet. And the EMF detector went nuts! We need to get this back to the shop to see what we caught!"

"Give him a minute," Elena's voice scolded, but I knew she wanted to know what I'd seen and what Hannah had captured, too.

"Hey, X." Jason swallowed and crouched on my other side. "I saw something."

My eyes met his, and I didn't see any of Jason's normal mischievous fun. What I saw was fear.

Frank moved us to the front of the café—away from the creepy back kitchen—and wrapped me in an emergency blanket that he kept bundled in his work satchel.

"As soon as you passed out, I ran to get Frank and Elena," Hannah said, taking a sip of hot cocoa from the thermos Elena handed her.

"I was there the whole time, X." Jason's voice was still low, serious, despite having just chugged a gulp of hot chocolate himself. "I saw the outline of a little girl, then this big, dark shadow blotted her out and covered you. That's when you started to cough. You were burning hot." Jason's voice choked up, and I swear I saw tears in his eyes. "I—I thought..."

"But we didn't wait. Jason knew something bad was here and my gear was going nuts. So, we threw holy water on you." Hannah squeezed Jason's shoulder.

Jason seemed to come back to himself then. "Right. And the shadow person went away. Then you woke up."

"Leaving your new apprentice to fend for himself, are we?" A cold, twisted voice slithered from the doorway, making me shiver more.

It was Mr. Gallows, the chief of operations in charge of the New Orleans Office of Psychic Intervention. The frigid-eyed, deathly pale-skinned man I'd first seen at Madame Monique's stood peering in the doorway at us. The one who looked like some sort of vampire, and who Madame Monique had warned me about.

"Randle," Frank's voice rumbled low in greeting, neither his lips nor eyes smiling. "Aren't you *in charge* of the hospital investigation?"

"You know very well that I am. But that's no longer your concern, is it? *All* of New Orleans is my charge. And this," he gestured around the husk of the café, "is part of it. Which means you need to tell me right now why some..." He sniffed as though he'd smelled a piece of rotten fruit. "Some paranormal investigator in training had to run off to find you when *your* apprentice was in trouble? Why was he lying in the middle of the floor coughing?"

A boulder-like weight settled on my chest. Just how much had Mr. Gallows heard? Madame Monique had said he was not happy that Frank had pulled strings to become my mentor, and had prevented me from getting shipped off to some special school for unusual psychics. If Mr. Gallows found out I was showing signs of this new, rare ability, the Sight, I don't even know if Frank could stop him from taking over my life.

I coughed again and spoke before anyone else could. "I'm allergic to smoke. Asthma attack, and I forgot my inhaler." I felt bad for lying—almost. Gallows was so creepy that a little lie to protect Frank seemed forgivable.

Gallows narrowed his gaze on me. Dark eyes glinting dangerously. He took a long stride toward me. "That doesn't explain why I saw him entering this building with his school friend." He eyed Jason skeptically, then swung his gaze to Hannah. "And his Pretender cousin."

Hannah flinched, but gritted her teeth. Being called a Pretender wouldn't make anyone happy—especially not Hannah—who understood she wasn't psychic but loved working with equipment to get a better understanding of the paranormal.

Frank started to speak, but I jumped up a little too quickly and might've fallen if Jason hadn't caught me. "That's my fault. Frank wanted us to check out the new fire scene first, but I wanted to come here. They were just around the block. So, I convinced my friends we should come here and do some work on our own," I rambled, continuing my white lie. "Uh, I wanted to get ahead. Show him what I can do."

His eyes were as narrow as the slits of a viper's pupils. "I see. In that case, Mr. Martinez," he turned on Frank, "you'd better wrap up your work at the hospital and ensure you get a better handle on your apprentice. Or I will." The last three words came out in a hiss that made my breath catch in my throat. He turned on his heel and walked out of the ruined café door without a backward glance.

The last thing on earth I wanted was to be mentored by Mr. Randle Gallows.

"Don't you worry about Gallows," Frank growled like a wolf who was on high alert, his eyes never leaving the back of Gallows's pale blond head until he was long out of sight. "You focus on your studies and your apprenticeship. I'll deal with him."

Elena looked from me to Frank and back, her fingers lingering a tad too long on the beaded necklace of protective gems she always wore. "Right. Frank will deal with Gallows. What we need to do now is find out what's causing unrest among these spirits and who or what is causing these fires. Hannah, let's go back to the shop to analyze your findings."

"While you do that," Frank said, "Jason, Alex, and I will go back to the apartment. Monique has something new she wants Jason to try and Alex and I need to work on helping him block his mind from unwanted spiritual attacks."

"Block my mind?" That didn't sound fun.

"It's something we usually cover when you're older and a fully certified apprentice, but *you* need to learn it now."

I'd never been so happy to be at Solomon's Eye, tucked snuggly in the back corner of Madame Monique's café-shop, surrounded by iron and more wards and spells of protection than any other place in town. Having the two bubbling hot pizzas in front of us was nice, too. One for me and Frank, the other for Jason.

"What's this?" Jason asked, talking through a too-hot mouthful of pizza. He lifted some sort of metal horn-shaped instrument up and tried to peer through the tiny hole at one end. The other end, a larger hole, was aimed directly at me.

"Point that thing somewhere else," I griped, shoving the horn so it aimed at the wall instead of my face. I was tired, hungry, and more than a little freaked out by the evening's events.

Madame Monique put a gentle hand on Jason's arm, so he lowered the horn. "It won't harm you, child," she spoke kindly to me. "But I know you've had quite a day, so I don't blame you for your concern."

"What is it?" I asked, not wanting to admit I felt relieved that the weird-looking horn was no longer aimed my direction.

"And more important, what does it do?" Jason asked after he swallowed his steaming mouthful.

"It's a Spirit Horn, and—" Madame Monique began.

Jason opened his mouth to shove in another bite, but Madame Monique stopped his hand. "Fill yourself with answers first, food later."

Jason frowned, but left the next piece of pizza where it was, still steaming in front of him.

"It is modified from the Victorian ear trumpet," Madame Monique continued.

Jason and I both looked at her like she was speaking a foreign language, then a memory of something I'd once seen on TV popped into my head. "You mean like one of those horn-thingies people used to hold up to their ears if they were deaf?"

I took a nibble out of my pizza. Jason glared at me, then gazed hungrily down at his own. Madame Monique quirked her lips, but said nothing—probably because I hadn't talked with a mouthful of food.

"Yes, child. It is much like those 'horn-thingies' except this one has been modified with seals and wards to help amply the voices of the dead. It will, if it works, help Untouched and psychics alike hear what ghosts are trying to tell us."

Jason's mouth fell open into an O, and I was totally glad it wasn't stuffed with partially chewed cauliflower-crust pizza. "So, this is the device you were having me do research for?" The pizza now forgotten, Jason held the horn in his hand like some sort of sacred treasure. He ran his fingers along the carved inscriptions. "I found this symbol. It's Egyptian and is supposed to help tune into the spirit realm. And this one." He pointed out a swirly symbol to me. "This one amplifies sound."

Madame Monique smiled at him. "I told you your work was important, *mon kè*." *Mon kè* was a Haitian saying that Madame Monique reserved especially for Jason. Jason didn't seem to mind. I think he sort of liked feeling special. And with Madame Monique, he was special. He was her assistant now every day after school and on weekends.

"Be careful, Monique." Frank spoke so softly I barely heard him. "I know Randle Gallows comes here for supplies, but I wouldn't show him too much of what you do."

"No, *mon ami*. I will not. That man is powerful, but not to be trusted."

Frank gave her a firm nod. "That he is not."

The next morning, Frank sat me in the leather chair facing his desk. This was not how I'd planned to spend Halloween. Hannah had wanted us all to go trick-or-treating tonight, and I didn't even have a costume. I was going to use some money Frank had given me as a stipend, as he called it, and buy something today. But there was no time for that now.

I usually liked to sit here and read or listen to him teach me about the different types of entities, but I had a feeling this time was going to be different.

Frank pulled a brick-size, heavily warded iron box from his satchel and set it on the edge of his desk. "I've brought something here in hopes of helping you remotely contact Alice."

"Here? You want me to bring Alice here?"

He tapped the box. "Inside this ghost trap is an original piece of wood from the café. It still has char marks from the Great Fire."

Sweat immediately broke out along my forehead and I felt like I might puke. "I thought you said it was important never to bring items from a haunted site home because they could follow us? Just like what happened to me with Mr. Wilkes when I left the key in my pocket." Mr. Wilkes had attached himself to me through the key to his basement door, which I'd accidentally left in my pants pocket. After that, there'd been no stopping him. Once he'd found a way inside my house, I hadn't been able to get rid of him until I crossed him over.

"It's not something I would normally do," Frank said behind his desk, the box sitting ominously between us. "But under the circumstances, I think it's the best way to help you harness this new power we've seen surfacing. If you have the Sight, and if we work on it here, this is a more controlled, safer environment. If things get too out of hand, I can put the wood back in the box and, theoretically, cut off the ghost's contact with you."

"Theoretically?" I squirmed, and so did Frank.

"It's not something I've ever tried, but it should work. At least it's the best way I can think of to help you learn to control your abilities. If you can learn to talk to Alice without her taking over all of your senses, then you'll have better control. And with control you'll not only be safer, but can also get more information to help her cross over."

Frank rose from his chair and perched beside the spirit box on his desk. "So, I'm going to open this on the count of three. But before I do, I want you to focus on the chair beneath you. What does the leather feel like beneath your legs? Beneath your fingertips? What does it feel like knowing you're here. Safe in my office at home."

Home.

That word plucked at my heart like a guitar string—melodic, but slightly out of tune. True, I lived here. But was it home? Part of me said yes... the other part wasn't so sure. I missed Dad sometimes. But he wasn't a big part of my life before the accident. Mom was. Mom had been home. Dad lived in my old house now, but it wasn't home anymore. I pushed away the painful thought, glad I had Jason and Hannah and my new studies. Besides, there wasn't really time to think about how I felt about this place right now—home or not. I needed to focus on learning to control whatever new crazy psychic gift I might have.

"Alex." Frank waved a hand in front of my face. "I need you to focus. You have to focus." He ran his hand over his scruffy beard. "Under better circumstances things wouldn't be progressing so fast, but with this outbreak and Gallows—"

"No, it's fine. I'm okay. I can do it."

He studied me for a moment, then nodded. "Focus on the chair. Once you do that, then focus on Alice. Call to her. If her connection to the building is strong enough, then we may be able to summon her here with this piece of her home."

There was that word again. Home. Maybe it had power. I shrugged it off for now. "Right. Focus on the chair..." I wasn't convinced this would work, but I supposed it was safer to try to talk to Alice here than when I was actually in the place where she died.

Frank placed a hand on the box. "Ready?"

I looked at him, totally unsure if what we were about to do was a good idea, then sighed. He was my mentor. My teacher. He was becoming my friend. It was his job to help me learn to control this, and my job to learn. So, I took a deep breath in through my nose and out through my mouth like Dr. Midgley had taught me after the accident, then closed my eyes. "Ready," I whispered.

Deep breath in. And out. In. And out. I felt myself relaxing into the chair. Felt the weight of my butt and slightly stiff hip against the seat, and where the edge of the chair pressed against my thighs. My hands rested on either side of me and I pressed my fingers into the cool, soft leather. I was anchored to the chair. That's what I needed to remember. Keeping it in the back of my mind, I opened my senses.

The room was quiet, empty. I listened harder. The soft silence was soothing to my ears.

"I'm going to open the box now." Frank's voice was distant, as though he was at the end of a long tunnel.

The box creaked open.

I wanted to open my eyes. What if a ghost flew out? At least I'd see it coming.

"Keep your eyes closed and stay anchored to the chair." Frank's voice was soft, but firm. How had he known what I was thinking?

So, I kept my eyes closed and listened. At first, there was nothing. No sound at all except for the lonely *tok, tic, tok, tic* of the hall clock.

Then the whisper of a pattering crackle started. It was distant at first, but steadily grew louder. It sounded almost like rain. Rain? That didn't make any sense. The wood in the box had been scorched by fire. The sound grew louder and the temperature in the room began to rise along with my panic.

A faint hint of smoke curled in my nostrils and I realized it wasn't rain I heard, but the crackling of flames as they consumed wood. My heart rate sped up, thrashing my ribs. I didn't want to go back to that hellish burning memory. I wanted to open my eyes. I shifted in the seat and remembered the chair. I felt it beneath me, solid and safe. I was in Frank's office. In his house. Safe. I was anchored to the chair. And Frank was right there to help if anything went wrong.

I needed to focus on helping Alice. That's why I was doing this. I needed to set the trapped spirit of the little girl free.

I called out to her with my mind. *Alice.*

She's the one I wanted, not the fire. And definitely not that creepy convict or whatever he was that terrified her and tried to choke the life out of me.

Jaw clenched, I scrunched my eyes even tighter and imagined Alice. Her dark hair, white nightgown, soulful eyes. *Alice,* I called out again with my mind and senses. *Alice, are you here? Alice!*

A cool sigh wafted across my cheek like a winter breeze.

"Alice?" I asked aloud. I felt a bit ridiculous with my butt stuck in the chair and my eyes screwed closed, calling Alice's name aloud. What if she wasn't even here? I'd look like an idiot.

She sighed again and coils of goose bumps twisted up my arms.

"I'm here." I heard little footsteps patter around me as if she were examining the room. "Where am I? I want to go home!"

"It's okay, Alice. We'll take you back home. I just thought..." That was the trouble, I hadn't really thought it out at all. "Um, I thought it would be safer to talk here. You know, without him?"

The feverish chill of Alice was suddenly beside me, her breathing heavy. "Oh, but don't you see? You've brought *him* here, too."

My eyes flew open. There was no way I was going to sit here with my butt plastered to a leather chair and not see what was coming—no matter what Frank said.

When I opened my eyes, I saw I was still in the apartment, but it wasn't our apartment. It was as if Alice's house had been transposed on top of this one. The walls of Alice's house took the place of Frank's bookcases, but his desk was still there—right in front of me. Flames and smoke poured out of the iron box on the desk, and Frank was nowhere to be seen. I was in some sort of warped death memory. Well, maybe that was better than being in a full-on death memory.

Alice's sweaty fingers clenched my hand. "Don't leave me," she cried.

I squeezed her hand. "Don't worry. I won't. I just wanted to talk to you without any interference..." Only it looked like it hadn't worked.

A massive dark shadow began pouring out of the box before us like thick, smoky gas being poured into a man-shaped bottle. Slowly, I could make out the details of his form. Arms, legs, torso. Ragged clothes. A leg shackle? He was tall and broad. His heavy eyebrows were raised, his eyes slanted into evil slits. He stretched, and the flames licked up higher around him.

"What do you want?" My voice wavered, but I commanded it to be firm.

He looked around the room, and took a looming step toward me, the chain of his ghostly leg shackle making a metallic scraping sound against the wooden floor. "You've given me what I want."

Alice whimpered.

"And what's that?" I asked, pushing Alice's semi-solid body behind me so that I stood between her and this monster.

"You removed me from my prison. You've set me free."

Susan McCauley

CHAPTER NINE

"No!" My scream nearly split my skull. "Close the box!" I yelled, hoping Frank could somehow hear me from this nightmare memory world. "Close the box!"

The man narrowed his eyes and prepared to lunge. I felt my pocket for holy water and realized it wasn't there. Frank and I had been doing an exercise to help me learn to control my power—not to battle some evil ghost—so I hadn't put it in my pocket like I do before I go on a case. No holy water. No salt. No escrima stick. I was defenseless.

The ghost prisoner launched himself at me.

I ducked, wrapped my arms around Alice's cowering little body, and pulled her out of his way. The ghost prisoner went straight through me, but not before he wrenched the fire-charm bracelet off my wrist. I felt it break. Saw it soar through the air. Then it clattered to the floor. Searing pain shot through me, like fire and ice scalding my skin from the inside out.

Teeth chattering, I turned my frigid limbs to see where he'd gone.

He shot off the wall and something I couldn't see through the smoke crashed to the ground. He charged back toward me, but I yanked Alice sideways, away from the iron box. Away from the desk and windows.

Giving me an evil grin, he lifted a chair high over his head. I braced myself for a painful blow.

A hissy-yowl issued from the smoke.

The ghost prisoner's gaze shifted, and so did mine. Onyx leapt between us. His tail was puffed out like a massive raccoon's, and he looked about five times bigger than his normal size.

"Onyx," I croaked. He didn't even look at me, just stood his ground between me and Alice and the convict.

The big man studied the small house panther between us, then suddenly grinned. He shifted his gaze to the windows, and all at once I understood. He didn't want me. Not really. He wanted a way out!

I lurched toward him, trying to get past Onyx, but Alice screamed, pulling me back.

"I can't let him break the windows!" If he broke the windows, the wards wouldn't hold. He could roam the city to terrorize the living. Then he'd be truly free.

"Onyx, stop him!" I screamed, pulling to get free of Alice. Her fingernails tore at my skin like fiery claws, but I yanked my arm away and launched myself at the malevolent spirit. My injured hip shrieked in pain, and my leg crumpled beneath me.

Onyx let out a yowl when I fell and stood guard over me.

"Don't worry about me." My voice quavered with agony. "Stop. Him."

But there was no time. The man let out a long, cruel laugh, then launched the chair straight at the window.

I covered my head with my arms. Shards of broken glass rained down around us, making little slices in my skin.

Alice started screaming again. I opened my eyes and jumped up despite the searing pain. The iron box glowed amber and a whirlpool of smoke and fire twisted around us, sucking up everything ghostly in the room—trying to pull it into the iron box.

Onyx leapt onto my leg, digging into my jeans with his icy claws. Alice and I grabbed for each other, holding on as tight as we could. But it was no use. She was being pulled away from me by a ghostly gale. She clung to my arms, her hair whipping around her tear-streaked face, her legs floating parallel to the floor. Our fingers dug into one another, but it was no use. She slid down my arms until only our fingers were touching.

"Please," she cried. "Don't let go!"

"I'm trying not to!" I yelled over the raging wind and flames. But as I said the words, a torrent yanked her from my grasp and sucked Alice into the iron box in a swirling vortex of smoke and flames.

The next thing I knew, I was soaking wet and on my back staring up at the ceiling. I had a pounding headache and stinging arms where the glass and Alice's ghostly fingers had cut me. Frank hovered over me, his eyes brimming with concern. I couldn't move my head, but my eyes roamed the room. Frank's desk. Leather chair. Iron box, closed. Bookcases—with books blasted all over the room. Broken windows and shards of glass everywhere. No smoke. No fire. No ghosts. At least I was back in the present.

I wanted to say I was okay and tell him everything that had just happened, but all that came out was "ugh."

"It's okay. Just rest. I'm calling Elena." He wrung his hands and paced, never going farther than a few feet from my side.

"Ugh," I said again. My head throbbed with pain, and I wiped away several small droplets of blood that oozed from the cuts in my arms. "Onyx?" I croaked and tried to sit up.

"Don't move," Frank commanded, then placed a small sofa pillow under my head.

"What in Solomon's name just happened?" Mrs. Wilson floated into view, a dishpan in her hand.

"Where's Onyx?" I whispered, my voice urgent. I was unwilling to rest until I knew my friend was safe. "Is he?

Is he here?" What if he'd been sucked into the box? Could we get him out?

Merow. Onyx appeared at my side.

His tail was still slightly puffed, and his ears were back, but he looked unharmed.

"Oh, Onyx," I sighed. He jumped on my chest and purred, and I fell back against the pillow on the floor. "I'm so glad you were there."

"He was where, exactly? What did you see?" Frank crouched beside me, making notes in his mentor journal where he recorded how my studies were going.

"He was in a terrible place." Mrs. Wilson looked fretful. "I only saw the tail end of it. But by the looks of it, you two invited the fire inside our home."

Frank scrubbed a hand over his graying scruff. "Bad idea," he grunted and made another note. "I thought it would be safer this way."

"Hmpf." Mrs. Wilson gave us an indignant frown, which Frank ignored.

"Water?" I asked, feeling silly since I was soaked in the stuff. But my throat was parched, as if I had really just been at the scene of a fire.

"Oh, my. Oh, my. Oh, of course! Where *are* my manners?" Mrs. Wilson bobbed off to the kitchen to get me some water.

"What did you see, Alex? What did you learn?" Frank helped me sit up so I could lean against the sofa against the far wall.

I told him about everything that had happened in the fiery vision, or whatever it was. "And it looks like Mrs. Wilson and Onyx can see what I see. I guess that makes sense since they're ghosts."

"But a prisoner escaped?"

I started to nod, but my pounding head stopped me. He was a prisoner. Really. A ghost prisoner. Not just some innocent person who'd died in the fire. But really one of the men who'd been trapped and died in the prison. That couldn't be good. "Yeah. I think he is the ghost of a prisoner from the Great Fire," I whispered and rested my head in my palms. "That's why the windows are broken."

"I could see you interacting with something, but I couldn't see what. I thought I caught a glimpse of Alice a few times, but never the prisoner or Onyx or anything else." Frustration laced Frank's voice. "The room got very cold at one point. And of course I saw the books fly off the shelves and the chair levitate and get thrown into the window. But I didn't know who or what was causing it. That's why I closed the box."

A surge of gratitude filled me. "I'm glad you did. I tried to tell you to, but—"

"I couldn't hear you. Your expressions changed, but your mouth didn't move. You must've been talking to Alice and Onyx with some sort of telepathy."

"What?" That was the last thing I needed, some other crazy power.

"Don't worry, Alex. It's not uncommon for most Class A and B Psychics to communicate with ghosts through telepathy. I can do it, too, if I have a strong enough connection with an entity."

I sagged with relief. At least there was something normal about my ability.

A loud rap at the door jolted me forward, and my headache pounded harder.

"Alex! Frank!" Madame Monique flung open the door and led Aunt Elena, Hannah, and Jason into the room. Madame Monique took one look at me and her scolding eyes softened to a simmer. "Oh, child, what have you done?" She knelt by me and pressed a cool wrist against my too-warm forehead.

"Nothing." My voice cracked with anger and annoyance and a dash of fear.

"*We* were trying to help Alex learn how to better control being a Seer," Frank said. "I thought that by bringing a small part of the scene here, he could contact the ghost without being overwhelmed by the environment."

"And?" Madame Monique was like a feisty pit bull—sweet and cuddly when she wanted to be, but terrifying when she didn't. She rummaged in her multitude of skirt pockets and pulled out a small bottle. "I made up a batch of this just for you. I had a feeling you might need it." She glared accusingly at Frank.

He held up his hands and backed away, but I could see the trace of a smile on his lips.

She unstopped the bottle and two tiny tablets fell into her palm, which she offered to me.

"What—what is it?" I wasn't going to take some strange concoction, even if it was Madame Monique who made it, without knowing what in Solomon's name was in it.

"Nothing dangerous," Madame Monique smiled. "It's a mixture of peppermint, clove bud, laurel leaf, black pepper, cinnamon cassia, ginger root, juniper berry, chamomile, and thyme. It should help reduce your stress and the headache I think you're having."

"How did you know?" I asked. Jason said Madame Monique wasn't psychic, but sometimes I wasn't so sure.

"Oh, *mon cher*. I have worked with young psychics before. These headaches are not uncommon as you learn to use your gifts." She dropped two tablets in my hand, giving it a squeeze. "They will help."

"Um," Hannah interrupted. "That, and you've been rubbing your temples almost nonstop since we got here."

I took the tablets, immediately scrunching up my nose at the bitter-peppermint taste. At least there was peppermint. Otherwise they would've been awful.

Mrs. Wilson bustled into the room holding a tray filled with a pitcher of ice water, glasses, cups, and a pot of tea. "Water? Tea?" She floated around from person to person like a flying waitress. It must've been pretty weird for everybody other than me and Frank. We could see Mrs. Wilson. All anyone else could see were a tray and glasses floating around the room, but I guess they were getting used to that by now.

"Just water. Thanks." I took the glass and drained it immediately, thankful my most recent encounter with the fiery spirit was over—at least for now.

About half an hour later, I'd finished telling them what had happened when Frank opened the iron box. The whole time, Mrs. Wilson had been fussing in the kitchen, banging pots and pans and cabinet doors and doing who only knew what. A clink and crash sounded from the kitchen.

"What is she doing in there?" Frank stood up and strode into the kitchen to check on our friendly ghost.

"I'm so glad you're okay, Alex." Hannah moved from her chair next to me on the couch. "Your head is better now?"

"Way better." She smelled a bit like Madame Monique's lavender protection herbs. Maybe her shampoo?

"Good. So, I have news—I caught another good EVP. Elena and I couldn't make out everything, but it's the same man's voice. And this time I caught him saying *brûlez* over and over again."

"Great. So we know he wants to burn something. I wonder if he's causing the fires all over town?" I asked.

"He was trapped in the café till now," Jason said. "Could he set fires in other places?"

Hannah shrugged, but Elena looked worried.

Another slam of the kitchen cabinets along with the raised voices of Frank and Mrs. Wilson captured our attention. "This is more than enough, Wilhelmina!"

"But they're children. They'll be hungry!" Mrs. Wilson whined.

"They'll be fine. Let's go."

Frank looked annoyed and amused as he followed Mrs. Wilson into the room. She held a massive serving tray. On it was a plate of sugar cookies shaped like bats, pumpkins, and cats, all decorated in orange and purple and black sprinkles. There were even a few cute black cat cookies. There was also a plate of caramel apples and a dish of Rice Krispies Treats. "It's time for some nice cookies and Halloween treats, don't you think?" Mrs. Wilson beamed.

Jason lunged for the tray and sank his teeth into a caramel apple before Hannah had even made it off the couch.

Whoa—with everything going on with the fire ghosts, I'd totally forgotten that today was Halloween. Never thought I could forget the best holiday of the year. Unlimited candy? I used to make myself sick eating a ton before I even got home from trick-or-treating. Jason and Hannah and I had wanted to go trick-or-treating, but right now all I felt like doing was crawling back in bed. With my arms stinging, my head banging like someone had taken a gong to it, and a ghostly convict on the loose, I wasn't sure a fun night out was what I needed.

I frowned, studying a bare patch forming in the knee of my jeans. "Halloween's fun and all, but, um, shouldn't we stay focused on the case?"

"Nonsense." Elena gave a little stamp of her foot, and the look she gave Frank said they'd already had this conversation at least once. "Everyone loves Halloween. Even adults. I think you should all take the day off and enjoy the festivities—especially after everything you've been going through. The Halloween parade is tonight. You can catch beads. Candy. Go trick-or-treating. The OPI and Town Psychics' Office will be out to make sure things stay safe." Then she helped herself to an orange pumpkin-shaped sugar cookie.

Jason's eyes sparkled with hunger as he sucked caramel from his fingers. I could almost see him imagining all the candy he'd catch tonight from the people tossing it off the parade floats.

"I don't know." I eyed Frank guiltily, not wanting him to think I was shirking my duties as an apprentice-in-training, and not wanting my friends to know I didn't really feel like going.

Frank appeared to think things over for a minute, then nodded. "Elena's right. You need to enjoy the holiday. Besides, I think it'll do you some good to have a rest from the case before we get back to it. Let that medicine of Monique's work. Recover a bit, yeah?"

"Are you sure?" I asked, the pain in my head already seeming to fade at the thought of actually having a fun night out with my friends, even if the thought of crowds didn't thrill me.

"We won't lose anything by taking a well-earned day off. The case will be here tomorrow, and so will this." Frank gestured to the closed iron box on his desk.

Goose bumps snaked their way up my arms, and I shuddered at the thought of what might still be lurking inside. And what about Alice? She was trapped in there. Alone in her smoky world.

"I know what you're thinking, Alex. I know you're worried about the girl." He nudged the box. "But she's safe in here."

I jabbed my thumb at the broken window. "The convict is out there."

Frank frowned, then gave me a fatherly sort of smile. "I suspect he's too excited about his freedom to give you a second thought right now. I'll make some inquiries about him. You go and have fun tonight."

Jason smiled, grabbed a cookie, then groaned. "I wish we didn't have school tomorrow," he said and popped the cookie into his mouth.

Oh, yeah. School. Somehow I'd nearly forgotten about that, too. My head was a total scramble.

Sometimes I was jealous of Jason and Hannah getting to go to school. I actually sort of missed it.

Another thing that had changed since the accident. No regular school now. Just psychic stuff.

"You will come after school to help, *mon kè*," Madame Monique spoke firmly to Jason.

"And Hannah's going to start running the shop for me every day after school starting next week, right, Hannah?" Elena smiled.

"That's right." Hannah nibbled on a purple bat cookie. "That way the shop stays open while Aunt Elena is working on cases, I'll learn more about the business, and I can still get my homework done."

"Yes," Madame Monique smiled. "It is a good plan. But you must go to school." Madame Monique sounded like a cross between Jason's mom and grandma. It was obvious she cared about them. About us. A lot. "Just as I must get back to the shop. It won't run itself. Come by tonight before you go out. I'll see you have a good dinner." She smiled at us and gracefully swept from the room.

"Guys, this is my first Halloween in New Orleans. I hear the parade is amazing, and I don't want to miss it." Hannah put her hands together like she was pleading.

Frank slapped his hand on his desk in a very un-Frank playful way. "That settles it. Hannah can't miss the parade. Let's get this place cleaned up and I'll put some warded plastic shields over the broken window until they can be repaired. Mrs. Wilson?"

"Yes?" She floated merrily beside him, the tray in her hand.

"I'll take one of those Rice Krispies Treats!"

CHAPTER TEN

After stuffing ourselves with Mrs. Wilson's Halloween cookies and caramel apples and Rice Krispies Treats, Hannah and Jason had gone home to scrounge up costumes and I took a big nap. After experiencing a horrific fire and having a nasty spirit pass through me, all I wanted to do was sleep. Although the sugar had definitely helped my headache.

It's crazy what four extra hours of sleep can do. When I woke up, I was hungry again, my headache was a memory, and I was eager for a night out with my friends. I was actually feeling like my old self again. Well, almost.

I grabbed a pair of nearly clean jeans off the floor and pulled them on, followed by a fresh black T-shirt and a thin, black, zip-up hoodie. That was another amazing thing about having Mrs. Wilson living with us. We didn't have to cook or do laundry. I wasn't sure I'd want to stick around to serve other people after I died, but it didn't bother Mrs. Wilson. She actually seemed to like it. I hadn't had homemade sugar cookies since Mom made them last Christmas. Her last Christmas. The thought shot a pang through my chest, but I ignored it. Tonight was Halloween, and we were going to have fun. Mom would want me to. So that's what I planned to do.

I knew Hannah and Jason were bound to be disappointed with my costume choice—or lack of one—but I just didn't have the energy for all that. Besides, any costume-like clothing I had was at my dad's house, and I hadn't really seen him lately. Home wasn't home anymore, anyway. I shrugged off the sting in my heart. He was busy and so was I. It was fine. I had Frank, Elena, Madame Monique, Jason, Hannah, Onyx. I was good.

I met Jason and Hannah at Solomon's Eye at five o'clock sharp.

Hannah and Jason were already there when I arrived. It actually looked like they had been there for a while. Jason had probably come back to work with Madame Monique, and Hannah, not wanting to be left out, had come along.

Sage and lavender and myrrh filled the air, and I passed a small maze of wooden shelves strewn with books and trinkets as I made my way to the counter where Jason was inspecting the Spirit Horn he'd been working on with Madame Monique.

True to J's style, he was decked out in his yellow and green Jamaican soccer gear. He hadn't loved playing ghostball, or any other sports, but he loved his Jamaican football team. Hannah was floating around the store dressed like some sort of gothic grim reaper, a dramatic black hood draped over her head, plastic scythe in hand. She was inspecting the various herbs and potions and amulets that Madame Monique kept in stock at Solomon's Eye.

As soon as Jason saw me walk in, his face lit up. "Hey, X! Come and look at this." His excitement was so contagious it made me grin. Jason motioned for us to follow him to the little wrought-iron table we liked to use in the back corner of the room. "It's still under wraps, so we can't let any customers know what it's about just yet. But it's almost done," he whispered, excitement making his voice hitch.

I held the metal horn in my hands, looking at the decorative inscriptions and seals that were sprawled across its surface. "No electronics," I said, turning it over in my hands. That was one thing I'd noticed about the things in Madame Monique's store and her inventions. If she could avoid technology, she did.

"That's why it's perfect. No electronics like modern hearing aids. Do you know there's a record of a lady who used an early electric hearing aid with no wards...a ghost got in her head and scrambled her brains? It took over her body and everything. So, no. Madame Monique doesn't want us to use electricity, and after what I've learned, I agree. Besides, with some of her Haitian wards..."

"You mean magic?" Hannah wandered up to us, a strange, pensive expression wrinkling her forehead.

Jason shrugged. "Wards, sigils, magic. Things to protect us against the supernatural."

"But you say it's not witchcraft?" Hannah didn't look convinced. "I've just… I've been reading about witchcraft recently and it seems, I don't know, like…it can be dark. Scary."

"The word 'witch' means a lot of different things to a lot of different people depending on where they're from and what they believe." Madame Monique had done her usual appear-out-of-nowhere thing on us. She was good at mysteriously popping up. "Do I sell supplies that can be used for witchcraft? Yes. But many of those same supplies are used for herbal medicine or wards to protect all of us against malevolent spirits. So, you see, it's really about a person's practices and intent. It's what they do or plan to do with what they have that is important."

She pointed at the ceiling to a small space that didn't butt up under the floor of our apartment upstairs. "Do you see those?"

"The witch windows," I recalled aloud. I remembered Madame Monique telling me about them the first time I'd met her.

"Ah!" she smiled. "You remember. Yes. They are witch windows. They stop those with nefarious practices or evil intent from getting inside. They are not foolproof, but they help," she murmured to herself, then looked pointedly at Hannah, who squirmed under Madame Monique's intense gaze. "Those are the ones you think of as witches, Hannah. The ones who practice black magic. The ones who only want to use spells and magic to cause harm. I won't help them here. If someone claims to practice witchcraft, but has good intent, then I may help. Many who do so are herbal healers. Some, as you know, help provide special wards to psychics. They aren't all bad. It's good that you're reading. There is so much in the realm of the supernatural to learn. So much we still do not know. It's good that you and your aunt use your equipment to capture the essences of spirits."

"I still wish I could see them." Her words held the hint of pleading and a dash of pout.

Madame Monique patted Hannah's shoulder. "You do see them, child. In your own, special way. You see them through their energy. Through their voices. You can capture their essences to show the OPI that Untouched can help, too. Do not forget your own unique gifts." Madame Monique smiled. "Now let me go pop some pizzas in the oven for you."

"A whole one for me, please." Jason grinned.

Madame Monique gave him an I-can't-believe-how-much-you-eat smile, rolled her eyes, and swept to the back of the store.

Jason sighed, his grin gone. "You know some people think psychics are witches?" His voice was serious, as if he'd been giving the whole subject of witches a lot of thought, or had discussed it at length with Madame Monique, or both.

"I guess..." Hannah said, like she hadn't thought about it like that before and had to process it.

I squirmed. I didn't know if they actually thought we were witches, but none of my old ghostball teammates called me anymore. They certainly thought psychics were weird, or at least should be avoided if possible. But that's how most of the Untouched felt about us; we were a necessary evil to combat the Problem. They still blamed psychics for letting ghosts run rampant in our world, even though every living psychic that had been involved in the Great Unleashing back in 1900 was long dead. It wasn't *our* fault the ghosts were here; we were just doing our best to deal with them.

Jason went on: "Why do you think when some people see Alex and Frank coming down the road with their black coats and leather satchels, they move to the other side of the road?"

Hannah shrugged. "Ignorance?"

"Maybe sometimes. But most of the time I think it's fear. Fear of things they don't understand. They just think psychics are necessary to deal with the Problem. And Alex *does* have powers most other people don't. To them, that's scary. But it's also like a sort of magic, isn't it? Maybe that's what scares them."

"Maybe," I said. It was weird how what Jason was saying was making me think of stuff differently. "The wards we use are mostly based on religious texts. But I guess that's what religion is sometimes, isn't it? A sort of window into the supernatural."

"That's true, I suppose." Hannah's voice drifted into silence for a moment before she spoke again. "And you do have good intent, Alex. We all do. So whether it's magic or not, we are trying to help people and spirits."

"It's like Madame Monique said." Jason pointed to the packed store shelves around us. "She sells wards and herbs and charms to people with good intent, but she has nothing to do with black magic." He sounded like it all made perfect sense to him. I still wasn't much clearer on what witchcraft was or wasn't, but it sounded like it all came down to intent.

"Well, whatever it is, I'm glad she stays away from the dark stuff." Hannah took the Spirit Horn from me and gave it back to Jason. She shoved up the sleeve of her reaper robe and looked at her WardWing to check the time. "Hopefully, the pizzas won't take too long. We don't want to be late for the parade."

"Right. I'll go put this away, and I'll bring the pizzas back with me. Shouldn't take long. Madame Monique made them for us earlier. She just had to pop them in the oven." Jason took the Spirit Horn and scurried to Madame Monique's mysterious backroom where she and Jason did all of their work and inventing.

"So, what are we going to do about Alice?" Hannah asked. "I've been thinking a lot about her, and I'm worried that a little girl is trapped at the scene of her death. It's spirits like that who can go malevolent, right?"

"I'm worried about her, too, but not because I'm worried she'll go malevolent. Spirits usually go malevolent only if they were bad to begin with. Like that prisoner." I shuddered as I thought of his hulking shape forming before me and of all the damage he'd caused in the apartment. "I don't think she will. She's...she's sweet.

And I reread Frank's interview transcript with the café owners. They said that things have moved around the place on occasion—cups turned upside down, napkins had been blown across the tables, the radio station changed. Things like that, but nothing bad." I suddenly started wondering about the prisoner. "So, if the café is the site where Alice and her family lived, then why is the ghost of a prisoner there?"

Hannah twisted her lips in concentration. "Well, we know the jail was basically next door. Maybe since the walls burned down he can roam in a larger area?"

"Maybe," I said, but wasn't so sure. "But the café owner, who's had the place for over forty years, had nothing to report about bad feelings or bad things happening." I needed to think more about this and talk to Frank. "All I know is that he's very dangerous. And mad. So, the last thing I want to do is put you and Jason in danger—again. I think I need to work with Frank on this one."

"With Frank? What about us?" Her tone was mixed with anger and annoyance.

"I don't want to leave you out, Hannah, or Jason either. You both saved me back there. But you both could have been killed when I crossed over Mr. Wilkes, and Jason could've died and had his soul get trapped forever at Lafitte's Blacksmith Shop Bar if things hadn't turned out the way they did. I just can't put my best friends in danger like that again."

"You don't get it, do you, Alex?" Hannah gave me a soft smile, which surprised me. I thought she was going to explode. "I'm your cousin. And Jason and I are your friends, yes. But we're more than that. We're your team. We want to help you. We're here for you. It's just as much our case as it is yours, and we have your back. Always. If you have to face danger, then we'll be right there with you."

"But—" My heart sang with relief, but my head argued that it wasn't a good idea. Still, her words surged through my blood like a warm, comforting wave.

"But nothing. I want to be a professional paranormal investigator when I get older. Why do you think Elena is starting to let me run her shop in the afternoons?"

I sighed, knowing I wouldn't get another word in until she'd had her say.

"Because she's training me. She wants me to learn the business and know how to run the store. I think so I can take over one day. And it's what I *want*, Alex. I *want* to be a PI. I *want* to work with the paranormal. It's like Madame Monique just said. We all have our own unique gifts. I guess mine are in paranormal investigation. If I could leave school now to study the paranormal full-time, I would. I believe we can work together to make the world a better place. Safer." Hannah shoved her fallen reaper costume hood out of the way, leaned close, and whispered, "I haven't told anyone this, but I overheard her and Frank talking. He thinks she might be able to get a contract with the OPI. Our aunt Elena, the very first PI in league with the feds. It could change everything! Finally, the Untouched who want to help with the Problem will be able to work right along psychics."

Wow. That would be pretty amazing. "That would definitely change things."

"Of course it would." Jason plopped a pizza down between me and Hannah and another one in front of his spot, before sliding into one of the wrought-iron chairs. He took a massive bite, but kept right on talking, mouth stuffed to capacity. "And I'm going to learn what Madame Monique does so I can keep inventing and do my own thing to help with the Problem, too. Just think of it, X! You as a Certified Psychic, Hannah as a professional PI, and me with ghost glasses and a new way to hear spirits! Together we'll be unstoppable!"

New Orleans was a crazy, wild, vibrant city, but Halloween here was over the top. The streets were packed with people—despite the recent spiritual unrest. Adults. Kids. Ghosts. Many were in costume. Well, the living ones anyway. The people here loved to dress up. And the Halloween parade was always amazing. It was sort of like a spooky Mardi Gras.

Music trilled, and the crowd chattered with excitement as the parade rumbled into view. First were the zombies and chain-swinging swamp people on horseback. They were followed by dancing voodoo priests and priestesses, and then several marching jazz bands of skeletons. There were reapers and devils, fairies and angels. People dressed in sequins and neon lights. Some wore too little clothing altogether. *Adults.* I rolled my eyes and wondered what the ghosts from more modest times thought about the show.

"Oh, look! Look!" Hannah chirped. "Here come the floats!"

I barely remembered Halloween outside of New Orleans. I'd been five when my parents moved us here from Boston, and Jason had come here from Jamaica when he was six. But not Hannah. I'd nearly forgotten this was her first Halloween in the city.

I grinned as the first float came past. It had the bust of a huge, cackling green witch on the front. Straight out of a fairy tale. Definitely not the kind of witch Hannah had been worried about earlier. Next came one sponsored by the city's OPI. It was a ghost float, of course. Billowing ghost-like figures danced and bobbed from the float's front and sides. The crowd screamed in false horror and jumped high to catch the beads and candy that were tossed to us. More floats came with pumpkins and cauldrons, skeletons and pirates.

Jason had brought a trick-or-treat bag, which he was still busy filling, but the hammering music started nudging the headache I thought had disappeared.

Boom. Boom. Boom. The music pounded. Voices thrummed in my ears. People laughed and danced. Lights blinked. Nausea crept its way from my stomach to my throat, and my world spun.

Suddenly, I felt very cold. Too cold for an autumn evening in New Orleans. I looked up and saw—not three feet from me—someone who looked as if they'd been burned in a fire. At first I thought it was a fantastic costume, but the woman took a step closer and the cold coming from her turned my veins to ice. That's when I noticed she was translucent. A couple dressed like an angel and a demon danced right through her.

"Hey, Alex, you okay?" Hannah looked at me with a slight frown.

"I'm fine," I lied, grabbing onto the Nazar Boncuğu that had worked its way out of the neck of my T-shirt, silently annoyed with myself for forgetting to ask Madame Monique for a new fire charm.

"It's your head again, isn't it?"

I didn't respond at first, then gave her a tight nod. No point in lying about it—especially not to Hannah, who had an uncanny way of discovering the truth. Besides, that creepy, burnt-up woman swaying to the music, and her being here, was just making my head hurt worse— like fire and ice were dancing behind my eyeballs.

"Hey, Jason!" Hannah called out over the beat of the jazz and roaring buzz of people. "Let's get out of the crowd and maybe do a little trick-or-treating."

Jason lunged and grabbed another pack of candy that someone in a zombie costume had tossed off a passing float, totally oblivious to either of us.

"Ja-son!" She lifted herself on her toes, trying to get his attention. "We need to go."

"I don't know," he called out, not even looking at us. "The candy's pretty good here."

"Oh, for heaven's sake." Hannah dropped her hands against her thighs in exasperation. "I'll *buy* you some more candy!"

That stopped him in mid-lunge. "You will?"

She rolled her eyes. "Yes."

"When?" Well, at least she had his attention. If my head hadn't felt like a generator was buzzing inside of it, I would have laughed. Instead, I just pressed my hands over my eyes, trying to stop the pain.

The tattoos on my forearms that helped protect me from spiritual attack burned and another wave of iciness spilled over me, making me open my eyes. The fire-ghost woman was two feet in front of me. Staring straight at me.

"What do you want?" My voice cracked like a shard of ice.

Hannah bolted upright, immediately alert. She knew I was seeing something. "Jason. We have to go. Now."

The ghost woman just smiled at me, a reflection of ghostly flames flickering in her eyes. I swung around fast to make sure a building wasn't really on fire behind me. There was no fire. Only people. People and laughter and floats and candy.

My head pounded as if there were a sleet storm in my brain, and my stomach heaved as another wave of nausea overtook me. I would not throw up. Not here. Not on the street. Not in front of all these people.

The tattoos on my forearms and the back of my skull screamed with searing pain, and an icy hand locked itself around my wrist.

The ghost woman was holding me. Looking into my eyes. Silently pleading with me to help. Then the relentless pressure of the unforgiving darkness poured its weight onto me and I fell into throbbing blackness.

CHAPTER ELEVEN

The first thing I saw when I opened my eyes was the peeling white paint on a wall through the shadows of night. The soft sofa leather that smelled of old food and lavender pressed into my face. It was dark. Very dark.

"Where am I?" My voice cracked. I didn't think I was in the hospital. Hospitals were noisy, busy places. I remembered from the accident. It was really hard to sleep there. Nurses came in constantly to check my vitals, ask how I was feeling, give me medicine. It'd been exhausting. Here, it was quiet.

I heard movement, the sound of leather creaking beneath someone's shifting weight. "Dad?" I hadn't seen Dad much since I'd become a psychic. I knew the whole thing made him uncomfortable.

"No. It's me, Alex. It's Frank."

I sagged with relief. While I'd like to have seen Dad, having Frank here was somehow better. I knew he'd understand whatever was happening to me. And if he didn't, then he'd help me figure it out. Dad would have panicked and called 911. I stared at the spot where I heard

Frank's voice until I could make out his shadowed outline against the chair. "Why are all the lights off?"

I tried to sit up, but my pounding head forced me back into a lying position.

"You were sleeping." Frank creaked forward in his chair. "Monique put some medicine on you and told us to let you sleep."

Us? Then everything came crashing back to me. Halloween. The parade. Jason leaping for candy. The creepy ghost woman.

"What time is it? And how'd I even get back here?" I asked, forcing myself into a sitting position.

Frank flicked on a lamp and my eyeballs felt like eggs that might explode from the pressure in my head.

"It's nearly two o'clock in the morning. Jason and Hannah carried...er, dragged you here. It's good you weren't too far away or they would've skinned up your knees."

I looked down at my jeans. The fronts of my legs were pretty dirty and damp. They must've pulled me through some of the New Orleans street muck. Yuck. "Well, at least they got me home."

That word sent a quiver through my heart. Home. I thought of my room back at Dad's, but that wasn't home anymore. Not really. It hadn't been since Mom died. Maybe this was my home now. Here. With Frank and Madame Monique downstairs. And Jason and Hannah here every day after school. Home. The word echoed silently through my bones and into my heart.

"I said they should have taken you straight to the hospital!" Mrs. Wilson floated through the wall wearing her thin, floral housecoat, which is what she always wore. I supposed it's what she died in. I'd never asked, but it made sense because all the fire ghosts I'd seen were wearing burnt-up clothes.

"He's safer here." Frank's voice was harsh, and I knew he was stressed. "You know that, Wilhelmina. I know you've been listening to my conversations with Elena and Monique. The hospital is overrun with ghosts and they're spilling out into the community with the damaged wards. We're nowhere closer to solving that problem than we were two weeks ago. And the last thing Alex needs is to be surrounded by ghosts who can get in his head and show him their deaths."

"Oh, I suppose you're right." She wrung her hands and gave me a fretful frown. "But he was so pale." She floated over to me and laid a chilly hand on my cheek, which meant she was trying to comfort me, but it burned and made me flinch away.

"Oh. Oh, dear. I'm sorry. I didn't mean." Sparkling tears filled her eyes and made me feel like a total jerk.

"No. It's okay, Mrs. Wilson. It's just..." I reached toward her, but stop short of grabbing her chubby, translucent hand. I really wanted to take it. I knew she meant well. She'd been like a mother to me since Mom died. I didn't want to hurt her feelings. She was family.

"It's more painful when they touch you now?" Frank asked, like he knew the answer held a whole lot of something supernatural I didn't want to know about.

"Yes," I whispered. "It's always been...cold. But Mrs. Wilson's touch never *hurt* before." I ran my hands through my hair and yanked, wanting to pull the pain and frustration right out of my head. "What's wrong with me?"

"Nothing's *wrong* with you. You're still new to your gifts and you're discovering more about what you can do all the time. It's the same for all of us, but the biggest learning curve is when you're young." He looked at me with his I-can-see-into-your-heart gaze. "And you *are* young, Alex. But you've mastered a lot very quickly." He scratched the salt-and-pepper scruff on his chin. "Look, having a ghost touch you never feels good. But those with mal intent can make it feel like your skull's going to pop out of your skin. So, that's why it's so much worse when the bad ones touch us. As for Wilhelmina..."

It still made me want to laugh when Frank called Mrs. Wilson by her first name. *Wilhelmina.* True. She did live with us, but still...when we'd first asked him about having her move in, I thought he was going to have a heart attack.

He shook his head and sighed. "I think you're just ultra-sensitive right now because your ability as a Seer has just come through. Your interactions with them in the past...well, those death visions have made you more vulnerable. For now. But I'm working on something that may help. I just need to get approval."

"From the OPI?" I wondered if Frank was trying to push through another special request on my account. If it weren't for him, I would be at some psychic boarding school in a classroom full of kids two years younger than me.

He gave me a tight nod. "Your case is...unusual. So, they're being somewhat flexible, which isn't necessarily typical of the OPI. It's part of the reason Gallows is being so nosy about it."

I wondered what this thing that would help might be, but by the tight seal in Frank's lips, I knew that now was not the time to ask.

"We should get to bed. Get some rest." He looked at the still-closed iron box on his desk; the box that held a fragment of Alice's burnt-up home. "I'm going to do some more work with you tomorrow on helping control what you're seeing and feeling when you interact with ghosts. That way when we go back to the café tomorrow night—"

"Tomorrow night?" I gulped. I wasn't ready to go back to the café so soon. Not when I wasn't able to handle the Sight or whatever it was I was experiencing.

Frank studied me, eyes serious. "I don't think it's a good idea to reopen the box here. We need to keep the contents on site, where they belong. And we'll all be there to help you. Me, Elena, Jason, Hannah. If anything goes wrong, we'll pull you back. Too many people have died, and it's time to put an end to these ghosts and these fires."

I looked at my lap for a moment, trying to come to terms with having to go back into a fiery hell, but I knew I had to help Alice. We had to stop these ghost-related fires before anyone else got hurt—or killed. It wasn't fair to keep her trapped here. I gave him a nod.

"Right." He patted my leg. "Get out of those dirty clothes and get some sleep. There'll be a lot to do tomorrow."

Hot water splashed over my shoulders, running in comforting rivulets down my back and taking the chill out of my bones. The pain in my head had eased to a dull throb. I sighed and leaned into the water, letting it warm me to the core. If I could sleep here, I would.

Merow.

Onyx leapt up on the window ledge and peered down at me with a gaze that said he wanted to cuddle.

"Hey, Onyx. I guess I should turn this off and give you some attention, huh?" Like most cats, my ghost cat didn't like water. So, I enjoyed the warmth for a moment longer, then turned off the water and quickly grabbed my towel. If I could dry off and jump into my flannel pajamas faster than the steam left the bathroom, I'd stay warm.

I stepped out of the shower super fast and toweled dry.

Merow.

Onyx slithered past, rubbing my ankle and giving me a little love-nip. A shot of icy cold pierced my skin where he'd touched me. *Oh, no. Not Onyx, too. I have to be able to touch Onyx.*

I shivered, but forced myself not to pull away. If I did, he might not understand like Mrs. Wilson. And, ghost or not, I didn't want to lose my Onyx. Not now. Not ever.

"Hey." I pulled on my pajama bottoms before Onyx could circle back and make direct contact with my skin again, then rubbed my hair dry and donned a fresh T-shirt. The spot where he'd touched me felt like it'd been in the refrigerator for half an hour. I had to shake off this icy chill. "Want to go and get a cup of hot chocolate before bed?"

Merow.

Of course, Onyx didn't drink hot chocolate—or anything else for that matter—but having his company would help. Somehow things always felt less scary with him around, even if I couldn't cuddle him.

"Great. Let's go." I tossed my towel over the drying rack, and we headed out of the bathroom toward the kitchen.

Mrs. Wilson was nowhere in sight. Sometimes she disappeared. I always wondered where she went. Maybe back to Dad's to check up on him or watch one of her favorite game shows? Frank didn't have a TV here. Too dangerous, he'd said. That he had a computer was a big deal as it was, but he knew it was too important for work not to have one. So, he'd added every extra sigil he could find to the manufacturer warding. If anyone was safe from a spirit attack via the Internet, it was us. Frank gave cybersecurity a whole new level of meaning, which made sense since he had worked for a bit in the paranormal cybersecurity unit at the OPI.

I boiled some milk on the stove, poured it into my favorite mug—one from home that Mom had got me on a family trip to London a couple years ago—stirred in my favorite hot cocoa mix, and added a handful of mini-marshmallows. I closed my eyes and let the chocolatey steam waft into my nostrils. This was going to be so good. "My mom never let me drink hot chocolate before bed," I told Onyx, leading him to the kitchen table where I sat.

He leapt onto the table and settled next to me. So close I could feel the chill coming from his fur, but not so close that it hurt. "You'd better do that while you can. You know Mrs. Wilson won't stand for it." Mrs. Wilson hated it when Onyx jumped on the furniture—especially the table or kitchen counters.

I'd tried to explain to her that he couldn't drop litter or anything else on the counter. He didn't have dirt or bacteria or poop. He was a ghost!

"Cats do not belong on furniture," she'd huffed.

In response, Onyx had plopped down in front of her on the dining table, lifted his leg, and began cleaning his crotch.

Frank and I had howled with laughter.

Mrs. Wilson had scowled, then immediately disappeared through the kitchen wall.

Merow.

Onyx was watching me. I shrugged. "You know I don't mind you on the furniture."

Merow. He indignantly crossed his paws, one over the other, as if to say, *Well, I'm staying right where I am regardless of what you think.*

"I mean, it's a bit silly. It's not like you're going to leave fur in the food or on the table." I took another delicious sip that filled me up with warmth from my toes to my head.

Onyx just looked at me as if my discussing his traits of being a ghost cat was the most boring thing in the world.

"Well, I'm glad you're here." Hot cocoa in one hand, I tickled him behind the ears with my other and immediately snatched my hand back as though shards of ice had stabbed into my fingers.

Onyx tilted his head, ears perked, and looked at me quizzically.

"It's okay, boy," I said, wrapping my cold-snapped hand around my steaming mug. "We're going to fix that. Tomorrow." There was no way in the world I could keep going without being able to pet Onyx.

After finishing my cocoa and finally feeling warm again, I put the cup in the sink, rinsed it, and headed toward my bedroom by way of the living room.

Mrs. Wilson was still nowhere to be seen. Earlier, after Frank went to bed, Mrs. Wilson didn't say much to me except goodnight. I figured she was upset that she couldn't touch me right now, even though it wasn't my fault. She hadn't popped into the kitchen, and she definitely wasn't in the living room that doubled as Frank's office, library, and my study and combat training area.

As I passed by Frank's desk, I noticed the box, and goose bumps rippled up my arms, making my hair stand on end. Its iron lid was dull in the moonlight that shined through the windows, heavily etched with protective wards and symbols.

Merow. Onyx leapt up on the desk and looked from the box to me.

I swallowed the lump in my throat. "I know it's not fair that Alice is trapped here. But we'll help her. I promise."

Onyx nudged the box with his paw; it scooted closer to the edge.

He looked at me.

I scowled at him, not wanting to touch it.

He nudged the box again; it teetered on the edge.

"Don't you dare knock that off the desk!" Without thinking, I scooped the box up in my hands, fearing what might escape if it had crashed open on the floor.

Merow.

I shook my head at Onyx. "Right. I know it's fun to watch things fall. But not this." I sighed. "Well, I'll just have to put this someplace safer tonight so it doesn't end up open while I'm asleep. That would be a real nightmare."

Onyx padded silently after me into my bedroom.

My room was small, but not tiny. Enough space for a queen-size bed, one bookcase where I was beginning to grow my own paranormal library, a nightstand, dresser, and small wardrobe. Since it was a historic building, there were no closets. The wardrobe worked well enough. Being a psychic meant I got to wear a lot of jeans and black T-shirts, so I didn't really need to hang up too many clothes. And that was fine by me. I liked being comfortable, and in our line of work, we had to be. You never knew when you might have to bust out a wall and dig up some bones.

Onyx leapt onto the bed, gave me an innocent look, then curled snuggly at the foot of my bed. "Where am I going to put this so you don't knock it over?" I asked, squinting my eyes at him.

There was a small niche on my night table where I could squeeze the iron box between the wall, my lap, and my copy of *Elementary Psychic Studies*. I didn't like the thought of having Alice and, quite possibly, some other ghost lurking near my head all night, but having them tucked up in a box by my head was a lot better than them being out of the box and getting inside my head. Besides, I couldn't think of a better place to put them. Sometimes

Onyx roamed at night, but he never jumped on my night table.

I settled the box snuggly against the wall. Lamp on one side. Massive *Elementary Psychic Studies* book on the other. It should be safe there. I unclasped the Nazar Boncuğu from around my neck and set it on my bedside table like I did every night, tucking it up against the spirit box for good measure. I didn't like being without its protection, but I was at home in my own bed. And it could get annoying swinging around my throat while I slept. I'd tried, but sometimes I felt like I was being strangled.

Sitting on my bed, I stared at the box for a moment, wondering what was inside other than an old burnt piece of wood. Maybe just Alice?

Etched sigils glowed faintly in the face of the old windup alarm clock my mom bought me when I first learned how to tell time. It was four o'clock in the morning. Definitely time to sleep. I switched off my lamp and they glowed even brighter. I still missed Mom. A lot. But she was with me in so many ways. From the clock beside my bed to the picture on my bookcase. I was glad she'd crossed over. And even more glad I'd see her again one day.

My head sank into the pillow and I realized how tired I was. My headache was gone, but my body was heavy. I closed my eyes, feeling the blissful weight of sleep on my lids.

Eeee.

My eyes shot open.

Silence.

Eeee.

I sat up and looked at the foot of my bed. Onyx was still there, but sitting up, ears alert.

Eeee.

I looked to my right, my eyes skittering over my clock and book and landing on the iron spirit box. It had moved. Toward the edge of my nightstand.

Eeee.

It moved again, teetering on the edge. There was no ghost or presence in the room that I could see or hear or feel.

I sat up and reached out my hand to grab it...

Eeee.

Too late. Whatever was moving the box was faster than me. It tumbled off my night table and crashed open onto the floor.

Susan McCauley

CHAPTER TWELVE

Before I could scramble out of bed to put the charred wood back in the box, or call for help, the room filled with smoke.

I leapt out of bed, only to find the floor covered in pieces of wood and coated in glass and ash. Again I'd been transported into some sort of weird world that was the past projected onto my room. It was Alice's house and my room all at the same time, and it was blazing hot.

A cool hand curled itself in mine and I nearly screamed.

"It's okay," a little voice said. "I'm here."

I looked down to see Alice holding my hand, a smile on her partially charred face.

"How...how'd you get out?" My eyes darted around the floor for the box, but it was nowhere in sight.

She scrunched up her nose. "That's what that was? A box? It felt hot and tight and scary—like my house had been folded up on itself and put in an oven." Her lip quivered. "I didn't like it."

I squeezed her hand, realizing how bad an idea it had been for Frank to bring a piece of the past home with him.

I know he was just trying to help me learn. Just trying to keep me safe. But it had all gone so wrong and made a mess of his office and our living space. Not to mention how awful it had been for Alice. I guess even experienced psychics still made mistakes. Maybe that meant my goof-ups weren't so bad after all. Still, like Frank always said, we have to learn from our mistakes and move forward. We'd just have to find different ways of helping me learn to control the Sight.

"I'm so sorry, Alice. Frank, he's my teacher, he was just trying to help me learn to control how I..." Did she even know she was dead?

"How you can talk to ghosts?" she asked, her wide eyes brimming with tears.

I nodded with a tight-lipped smile. "Yep. That's my job. To talk with you and help you get to where you need to go. Wouldn't you like to see your parents again?"

"Uh-huh." She nodded, then sniffled. Her mouth began to quiver.

"It's okay. Don't cry. I'm going to help you." I put my arm around her. She felt solid. She was uncomfortably cool, but it didn't hurt me here like it had when I touched Mrs. Wilson or Onyx. It was like being in this weird ghost memory with her somehow helped make touching them more manageable, almost like I was part ghost. The thought made me shiver.

Alice tugged my hand, but wasn't looking at me. She was staring with wide-eyed terror at three enormous figures that loomed before us. "You can't help me," she cried, yanking me back toward the bed. "They...won't...let you."

Three hulking, shadowy figures blocked the doorway of my room, their forms silhouetted against a backdrop of glowing orange tongues of fire that leapt and danced around them. Smoke and the smell of burning hair and flesh nipped at my nostrils making me cough and gag.

One of the men took a single stride forward, his feet weighted down by the iron shackles that bound his ankles. Short lengths of chain ran up the sides of the figures' charred trousers, wrapped around their waists, then fell to the ground, ending with solid, iron balls so they couldn't run. How horrible it must've been to be chained up and burned alive in a prison. Chains and bars, heat and fear. I couldn't imagine the pain and panic they'd felt when they died. I didn't want to imagine. But I also couldn't let them keep causing harm. Their crimes should have died with them.

I stepped in front of Alice so she was between me and the bed, but she clamped onto my hand like a vise.

"You have to let go," I told her gently. "Just for a little bit." My voice sounded French when it came out of my mouth, but I understood it in English. So weird. As long as Alice understood me, I guess it didn't matter.

"But they'll hurt you," she whimpered, nearly breaking my fingers with her grip.

"I'm not going to let that happen." I gave her my best smile and rolled up my PJ sleeves so she could see my tattoos. I had protection. I could do this.

"Oh," she gasped, pulling away and looking down at the floor. "I don't like those."

"Don't worry." I crouched in front of her, my hands on her shoulders, ignoring the evil stares I could feel piercing my back. "They're not meant to hurt you. And I'm not going to let them hurt either of us," I whispered.

"Is that right?" one man scoffed, and I heard the clank of metal dragging against the floor as he took another step toward me.

In one quick motion, I stood and faced him. "Yes. That's right."

I grabbed for the collapsible escrima stick from beside my bed without even looking, thankful Jason had made me one small enough to stash in my room. I prayed it was there since this was my room, even if it didn't look like it. Would my gear travel with me into this warped reality? I had no idea, and I sure couldn't look for it through the billowing smoke.

My heart leapt with relief when my fingers wrapped around the metal stick. Usually cool to the touch, it was hot. The flames of this vision or whatever it was must be affecting my reality, too.

I extended the escrima stick with a flick of my wrist and stepped toward the ghost. "That's right. I'm not going to let you hurt her. I think you've done more than enough by scaring a little girl."

The man's smile turned to a snarl. "Let's see how you like it, bein' pent up in chains for years on end. Then burned alive. You'd give anything to have some fun. I want outta here like Alfred. He escaped and so will we."

I aimed my escrima stick toward his chest, ready to jab, when one of the other men lunged at me from the side, smacking his chain into my head. Pain burst behind my eyes. He pulled it tight; the metal was like icy fire as it slipped around my throat.

I gagged. Dropping the escrima stick, I tried to rip the chain from my neck. But it was no use. He just pulled—tighter and tighter and tighter.

My vision narrowed, getting darker and darker. His hand brushed my cheek and I caught a glimpse of glowing green. A pale hand. A green stone. I coughed and gagged.

Alice screamed. There was a burst of white light that swallowed the green.

Then darkness.

My eyes were crusted shut, my head throbbed, my clothes were drenched in sweat, and I was coughing up smoke. Either I'd just had the worst nightmare of my life or that spirit box had somehow managed to wiggle itself onto the floor and come open.

"Alex! Oh, Alex!" Mrs. Wilson frantically called my name, way louder than necessary. It sounded as if she were only inches from me.

I gently rubbed open my eyes. "Not so loud. Please," I whispered, hoping that the jackhammer in my head would stop pounding.

Mrs. Wilson was hovering about six inches from my nose, wringing her hands.

I forced myself to sit up. The world spun for a moment, then stilled itself. My throat was dry, parched. Swallowing stung. It was as if I'd really just been in a fire.

"I...I brought you a glass of water in case you woke during the night, but when I came in..." Her eyes were wide, fretful. She set a glass of water on my nightstand, and I noticed the iron box sitting closed on the floor near where it had fallen.

"Oh, Alex. There were these terrible men in here, and that poor, poor little girl."

"You could see them?"

Jaw clenched tight, she nodded so that her jowls wobbled. "Yes. Not as clearly as I see you and Frank. But they were here. They were trying to kill you."

She kept wringing her hands over and over again. That's when I noticed a black spot on her right palm. There was no way she'd closed that box. Iron hurt ghosts. It burned their essences.

"You didn't close the box, did you?" I asked, hoping she hadn't hurt herself on my account.

She held her chin up high and nodded toward the water. "I did what needed to be done. I wasn't about to let three ghouls hurt you and that poor girl. Not in my house. And not on my watch." The fierce, feisty Mrs. Wilson rose to the surface. The one who acted like a Louisiana black bear who'd do anything to protect her cubs.

"But the box. It—it...hurt you..."

She lifted a hand to touch my face, but stopped just shy of my cheek, a sad smile on her lips. "You're family, Alex. You're like a son to me."

Love and pain and confusion twisted in my heart. I cared about Mrs. Wilson. She was like family. But she wasn't my mother. I didn't want another mother. I had one, and she'd died. Nobody would replace Mom. Ever. I focused back on her injury to avoid the painful confusion in my heart. "But your hand's hurt."

She floated closer to me and lifted the glass of water off the table. "It's just a little burn. It will fade. In time. Now drink this." She forced the glass into my hands. "Your throat sounds scorched."

I tossed back the glass of water, then crawled to the kitchen for another. I was so thankful for Mrs. Wilson's help, but I didn't want her or any of my friends to get hurt because of me. And I knew that iron must have hurt her. A lot. And it was more than just a little burn.

"Alex. Where are you going?" Mrs. Wilson fretted over me the entire time. "I can get you more water."

I coughed up something black and tasted something metallic in my throat, then felt a slim trail run from my nose to my lip. Blood. I wiped it with my sleeve and dragged myself into the kitchen.

"Oh, Alex. Your nose is bleeding. This is not good. Not good. Shall I fetch Madame Monique?"

"No," I croaked. "Where's Frank?"

"He got called back to the hospital." Her eyes darted to the phone on the wall.

"Of course he did." Anger flared in my chest. He was never here when I needed him. He said I was his priority. He said being my mentor was the most important thing. Well, if that were true, why wasn't he here?

"Elena said it was urgent. You were sound asleep. He told me to keep watch over you, and that you should call if you need him." Mrs. Wilson sniffed, her tone defensive.

I groaned and hung my head in my hands, willing the pounding behind my eyes to stop. Nausea swirled in my gut. I swallowed another stream of smoky blood and forced away the urge to puke.

"Here. Have another drink." She lifted a chilled glass bottle of water from the fridge, but it suddenly slipped through her fingers and crashed to the ground, spraying me with icy water and shards of glass. "Oh, no. Oh, no. Oh, no. I'm so sorry!" Mrs. Wilson started to cry, her fierce demeanor shattering with the glass. "It's just I can't hold on to things very well when I'm upset. I lose my form."

"You don't need to be upset, Mrs. Wilson. I'll be fine."

"But look at you, Alex." She managed to float a tissue over to me so I could mop my bloody nose. "You're not fine." She rummaged around the kitchen cabinets, keeping busy to try to calm herself. "Frank left the medicine Monique made for you in here somewhere...I just don't know where."

"Would you stop?" I snapped. "Please." I tried to be nice, but I didn't want to be babied. I didn't want her trying to replace my mom. What I wanted was control. Control of these hauntings. Control of this new gift. Control of my life.

"No, I will not stop." Mrs. Wilson spun toward me, hands on her rotund hips. "I am here and I am going to help you use your gifts to the fullest. You can help so many ghosts cross over, but you are most certainly NOT going to kill yourself while doing it!" She sniffed. "With power comes pressure. Well, you've got a new power and you're not even close to learning to manage it. I've heard you and Frank in there practicing. I've *seen* the things that come to you from the memory of that wood. Awful things. And I'm not going to float around happily humming and making lasagna and cakes and gumbo while those—those nasty spirits batter your brain and give you bloody noses."

"Well what if I don't want this new power, huh? What if this stupid psychic power I got when my mom died was more than enough?" I spat.

"Watch your words!" She spat back.

"No. I'm not going to watch my words. I'm not going to do what you tell me to do. You want me to use my gift? Then why won't you let me help you cross over, huh? Tell me that?" Tears sparked in her eyes, but I was too mad to care. I was mad that Alice was trapped in an awful, repeating death of smoke and flames. Mad that I didn't have control of my powers. Mad that these ghosts were hurting me.

"You need a mother," she sniffed.

"I had one!" I yelled, hauling myself to my feet, my head pounding harder than if a jackhammer were tearing up concrete.

She gave a heart-wrenching gasp. "My boy Jamie would never have talked to me that way. Ever."

"Well, I'm not your boy. I'm not Jamie!" I screamed, not caring now if Madame Monique heard me. I was tired of trying to be something I wasn't. I wasn't her son. I wasn't being a good friend. I wasn't a full apprentice. I was just me. A kid who'd lost his real mother in a terrible accident. A kid who hadn't wanted to be psychic. Who hadn't wanted some extra, rare special power. But I was. And I was doing the best I could to deal with it. I just wanted everyone to leave me alone.

I stormed back into my bedroom, running into walls on my weak legs, leaving Mrs. Wilson weeping in the kitchen. I felt like a total jerk. I was a total jerk. I shouldn't have said all of those nasty things, even if they were true. Mrs. Wilson was trying to help me. She'd *saved* me from those prisoners. But I was tired of being helped. I just wanted to handle my problems on my own. Was that a bad thing?

I wrapped the iron spirit box snuggly in a towel and shoved it under my nightstand where it couldn't get knocked over, then grabbed the headache medicine Madame Monique had concocted for me from where I'd stashed it and took two tablets. Hopefully a peaceful, dreamless sleep would do me and my head some good.

Several hours later, I awoke to the whispering hum of silence. No voices. No kitchen clatter. No ghosts. I shut my eyes and sighed. There was a small crust of blood on my nose, but no more bleeding. And the pounding in my head had been reduced to a mild ache. It was nothing I couldn't handle. Still, it would have been nice if Frank had been here to help me. A knot of guilt coiled inside my gut. I hated that I'd been so mean to Mrs. Wilson. She wasn't my mom. She never would be. But she cared. And if I thought I didn't need people who cared about me, I'd be lying to myself. I needed to apologize before I did anything else.

I glanced over at my old windup alarm clock. It was just past five o'clock in the evening. November 1. All Saints' Day. The Day of the Dead. Maybe it would be the day I could send Alice to be with her parents. Well, if I was going to try, I'd better get going. I now had less than thirty minutes to dress, eat, get my satchel and supplies together, and get down to the café to meet the team for the investigation.

I wished Frank was here. He could teach me more about the Sight. Or could he? If it was rare, maybe he really didn't know that much about it. And he had brought the piece of Alice's house here to help me hone my skills, but that seemed to have made things worse. Frank was a famous OPI psychic investigator, but maybe he didn't know as much as I thought he did. That idea both scared and comforted me. If he still made mistakes at his age, then maybe my mistakes weren't so bad. But if he didn't really know how to help me with the Sight, I was in real trouble.

I just hoped that Mrs. Wilson hadn't talked to Frank yet. Not before I could explain what had happened and apologize to Mrs. Wilson for being so mean. This was one time I was glad Mrs. Wilson couldn't manage the phone because of electrical interference. Frank had enough on his plate, and I didn't want to make him feel worse for not being here when I needed him.

After yanking off my sweaty flannel PJs, I pulled on a clean pair of jeans and a long-sleeve T-shirt, took two more of Madame Monique's tablets, and snarfed down two orange pumpkin Halloween cookies. The pain in my head had settled to a minor thudding.

I drug a comb through my untidy brown hair and was startled at the person looking back. It was me, but I'd changed. My face was thinner, paler. I looked older. More serious. I wasn't just a kid anymore. I was a psychic. And soon I'd be a fully Certified Apprentice Psychic. I secured my brilliant blue Nazar Boncuğu around my neck and it gleamed against the chalky skin of my throat, making me feel safe.

Just then, a nebula of cold collided with me, goose bumps coursed up my arms, and I jumped. Then, I nearly screamed when Alice's partially charred face appeared staring back at me.

"How did you get out of the box?" I asked, worried there might still be a prisoner ghost waiting to attack.

"When the fat lady closed the box, I hid." She was so innocent, so sincere, I wanted to laugh that she'd called Mrs. Wilson "the fat lady."

"That was Mrs. Wilson."

Alice nodded solemnly. "She saved us."

"She did."

"And you were so mean," Alice said to me.

Tears of shame and regret burned my eyes.

Alice's chin fell and her mouth quivered. "I miss my mama."

Shoving back my anger and upset at myself for being such a jerk, I gave Alice a tight nod. "I know. I miss mine, too. But I'm going to help get those mean men to cross over so you can see your parents again. Okay?"

Alice's eyes sparkled with wonder. "Really?" A smile broke her glum face, making the creases in her charred skin crack open to reveal white ooze beneath. I did my best to hide my disgust.

"Really."

"You promise?"

I swallowed, knowing I would do everything I could to keep the promise I was about to make to this little girl. No one deserved to be burned alive and then separated from their parents for centuries. No one. "I promise."

Now, I needed to protect myself and get ready to meet the team so I could keep the promise I'd just made. I grabbed the holy water on my dresser and unstopped it with a shrug. I splashed a bit on myself to make sure I was awake, and to give myself extra protection. Alice winced when a droplet landed on her, but she was still there and I was wide awake.

She tugged my hand, sending jagged ripples up my arm. When I wasn't seeing her in the past, her touch was just as painful as Mrs. Wilson's. That was not good. I pulled my hand away gently and rummaged around in my dresser for the single pair of winter gloves I had. I'd probably look a little strange in autumn weather wearing gloves, but who cared if it saved me from the bone-chilling cold of a ghost's touch.

"I'm supposed to meet my friends at the café. You can come with me. I'll take you home, then Frank will help me, and we'll send you to your parents, okay?"

She shook her head no and stared into the distance as if she was seeing something on another plane that I couldn't see.

"Why not?"

"I need you to come with me first." Her brows drew together, her expression troubled.

I sighed. I really didn't want to go anywhere with a ghost. Especially not without Frank.

"Come, now." She grabbed my hand again and pulled, urgently. This time, instead of a sharp, cold pain, I got only a dull, cold ache. The gloves were working.

"Okay. I'll come with you, but let me leave a note." I let go of her hand to grab a pen and paper off the edge of my dresser, but Alice let out a wail so loud I had to clamp my hands over my ears.

"No! Now!"

"Okay," I called, ears still firmly covered. "Stop screaming. I'll come."

Her screaming ceased, and she quickly disappeared through my bedroom wall. I hated it when they did that; it made it so much harder to follow. I tugged on my last boot and raced out the front door after her. Hopefully Frank would know something was wrong when I didn't turn up at the café. I just hoped he could find me.

Susan McCauley

Chapter Thirteen

lice was moving fast. She was waiting on the corner of Royal Street and Ursuline Avenue when I came out of the apartment building. Madame Monique was nowhere in sight, or I would have yelled for her to tell Frank I was leaving.

We made our way down Royal Street, then turned left on Saint Ann Street, heading toward Jackson Square when I saw smoke. It was just a thin wisp twisting like a charred finger into the air, but I knew there must be another fire. I sped up my pace, jogging to keep up with Alice. We were close to the café, but she didn't go there. Instead, she stopped and went into the Cabildo. The site of the old jail.

Tourists were milling about out front, snapping pictures. A line of people trailed out the door of the St. Louis Cathedral, likely waiting to light candles for recently departed loved ones since it was All Saints' Day. Others strolled in front of the museum and the square, all blissfully unaware that a gnarl of smoke was rising from the building.

As soon as I set foot in the museum, the fire alarm sounded. People started screaming. Some ran. A security guard called for calm and tried to usher people outside. But I ignored them all and followed Alice into the smoky bowels of the burning building.

We ran through an open corridor filled with New Orleans artifacts, scurrying people, and thick smoke. The brightly lit halls quickly faded, transforming into a dimly lit wood and brick jail of the past. There was no evidence I was still in the twenty-first century. Gone were the electric lights. Gone were the finely polished wood floors. Gone were the fire truck sirens I'd heard in the distance. Instead, I heard bars rattling and cries in overlapping rough-voiced French and Spanish that I somehow understood.

"Help!"

"Let us out!"

"Help us!"

"Don't leave us here!"

Alice kept walking. Deeper and deeper into the jail. Soon we were in a hallway of jail cells. Figures packed the cells. They cried and pleaded for help. Some screamed. Others raged.

The stench of body odor and excrement hit me in the nose, making me gasp. I tried to hold my breath, but it was no use. I pulled my shirt over my nose and mouth and breathed. That seemed to help—a little. The floor was made of packed earth. There were no windows. Only bars and walls. Dimly glowing lanterns were hung at intervals along the narrow hall. Smoke billowed into the dark, dank chamber as if it were an oven filled with burning food. Where was Alice taking me? And why?

I began to cough. The smoke coiling and twisting itself into my clothes and hair and nostrils. I could barely breathe.

"Please!" A man's desperate, translucent face appeared through the bars to my left, making me leap sideways, nearly colliding with a wall. "Please," he begged again, grasping onto the bars until his knuckles were pale. His knuckles weren't just white. They were bones. One brown eye gazed down at me, pleading. The other eye had been burned from its socket, half his face charred.

My stomach churned, and I turned away. "I have...to help...them," I gasped to Alice, but she didn't stop until she reached the end of the hall.

I didn't have my work satchel. I didn't have Jason or Hannah or Frank. I didn't even have their bones. I had a packet of emergency salt in one pocket and a bottle of holy water in the other. That was it for supplies. I'd been so stupid to follow Alice without getting my bag or telling anyone where I'd gone. Had I walked into a trap?

Think. Think. Think! What could I do? What did I know that might help?

The standard prayer of crossing over only worked if we could bury the body. I doubted any of the bones were left here. Maybe some had been buried long ago. Or maybe they'd been consumed in the fire. What could I do? I stopped to think, trying to breathe. If I had my supplies and my friends, then we could cross over the prisoner ghosts who were trapped here. Without them, it was no use. I had to get out of this smoke. Once the firefighters put the fire out, we could come back and put these spirits to rest.

I turned to go back the way I'd come, but Alice immediately started screaming in agony. I covered my ears and took a step back toward the hallway exit. "I'll come back," I yelled over her long, piercing screams.

"No!" Alice was in front of me now, her mouth contorted into a growl of fury. She was no longer the little girl I was trying to save, but a fierce, terrifying ghost.

Cold rolled off her like a puff of breath in the winter, forcing me back toward the cells and the ghostly prisoners. I didn't want to have to use holy water on her. It would burn her essence. And she'd already felt enough pain. I held up my hands, hoping to calm her, praying she wouldn't try to get inside my head and make me see her death again. "Alice, stop. Please."

The keening wail that had been coming from her stopped. Quiet. Innocent. "You don't understand," she whispered. "You can't go. You have to stop him. Or he'll keep doing this. Others will die."

"What do you mean?"

She tugged on my gloved hand, sending mild numbness into my fingers, and pulled me forward. "Here. There's something here. They've been whispering," she said, her eyes traveling over all the poor souls still trapped in their cells after so many years.

"Something's here that's keeping them, and making them do bad things. Making me do bad things, like bringing you here." Tears flooded her eyes, but it all began to make sense.

"The fires. They're the ones starting the fires, aren't they?" I risked a look into the cells and was met by charred faces and empty eye sockets. There must've been twenty of them. And they'd all been burned. Alive.

Alice shook her head. "Not them," she said of the gray figures behind the bars. "Them." She nodded toward the end of the hall.

I turned toward the hulking forms of the prisoners I'd seen in my room. At their head was the one who had escaped at the apartment, the one I think they'd called Alfred.

He leered at me. A green light from the floor near the wall illuminated the chamber, giving his translucent form an eerie glow. He seemed to grow as he stood there, his form becoming more solid, more real. The power radiating from him grew stronger each second. "Stay back!" he snarled. He held his ankles before the green light, the shackles absorbing the power. The ghostly metal turned greener and greener, as if being flooded by some sort of supernatural power, until finally, it melted from his ankles and he was truly free.

I had to think. And think fast. I yanked the holy water from my pocket, but he knocked it from my hand and tossed me into the wall. I collapsed to the floor, my body a mass of aches. He raised his hands and the green light from the floor burst out like rays from the sun, and each of the jail cell doors flew open.

As one, ghostly bodies surged into the hall, surrounding me in a wave of icy mist and smoke and charred flesh.

"Alex!" Hannah's voice rang out from the entrance to the block of cells.

Relief flooded my veins. Hannah and Jason were here, both crouched at the entrance to the cell block. Headlamp on, Hannah held her EMF detector in one hand and EVP recorder in the other. Jason wore his spirit glasses, his head haloed in the smoky blue light that shined from them. He held the collapsible escrima stick he'd made for himself in his right hand and the spirit trumpet in the left.

If I hadn't felt like I was going to die from smoke inhalation, I would have jumped up, run through the painfully cold mass of ghosts, and hugged my friends.

"Stay where you are!" Jason shouted. "You're surrounded." His single visible eye filled up the lens of the *specula spiritis*.

"I can see that," I gasped, then coughed. "But I can't breathe. We need to get out of here and come back." I got to my knees. Maybe I could crawl through the ghosts' legs. I didn't have any holy water, thanks to the ghost knocking it out of my hand, but I still had salt. That might be enough to help hold them back. Besides, their legs would be a lot less painful to go through than their torsos.

The prisoner who'd had his shackles melted free by that weird green light stomped a foot on my chest to hold me in place. "You're not going anywhere."

Alfred's ghostly toe inched toward my throat, stopping at my Nazar Boncuğu. He growled as if the amulet were more of a nuisance than something that would actually stop him. He snagged the toe of his boot beneath my necklace and gave it a quick yank with his foot. My Nazar Boncuğu soared through the air. It clattered to the floor somewhere in the smoky gloom, far out of reach. The prisoner ghost leered down at me, revealing blackened and missing teeth. Then he placed his foot back on my chest and pressed until his toe touched the exposed skin of my neck. Sharp-shooting ice-like pain streamed through my blood, making my head pound. A scream tore from my smoke-raw throat and my lungs burned.

"Let him go!" Through smoke-blurred eyes, I saw Jason force his way into the throng of ghosts with the iron-tipped stick.

"Jason! Stop! Come back! The firefighters are almost here. They can help," Hannah called, but took a few steps after him, the lights of her EMF detector flashing like Christmas.

Jason aimed the stick toward Alfred. He was still several feet away because a few of the ghosts refused to move, but Jason was relentless. "Let him go, now."

Alfred's boot shifted on my chest so that his toe no longer touched exposed skin, and the relief was immediate. My head still throbbed, but I wasn't in agony. I wanted to send Jason and Hannah away. I wanted them safe. But who was I kidding? They were here, saving me. I had some basic tattoos, but with my Nazar Boncuğu gone, I was nearly defenseless.

Jason was looking straight through his ghost glasses at Alfred and the surrounding ghosts, who were now more angry than amused. He held the spirit trumpet to his ear.

"I'll not have you or him or the girl thwart our escape. We will have our revenge on the people of this city!" Alfred roared. "They will burn as they let us burn!"

The crowd of prison ghosts grew suddenly restless, and the temperature of the air dropped despite the smoke and nearby flames. They began to press in on Jason. His eye bulged and he let out a strangled cry.

"Go, J! You and Hannah go get help!" My voice sounded as though it was being funneled through a tunnel of sandpaper, and my throat burned. I had an idea, but there was no way it would work if Jason and Hannah were trapped in here with me.

"I'm not leaving you, X!" Jason cried, but then Hannah was there, pulling him back away from the throng of ghosts that threatened to overtake him.

"The firefighters are just outside. He'll be okay. But we can't become victims ourselves." I barely heard Hannah's voice over the pounding of my heart. At least the ghost had taken his weight off my chest; his foot was still there, but barely. Flat on my back, I turned to my friends, willing them to leave. Smoke swirled and twisted around us—if it was real or part of some ghostly nightmare, I wasn't sure.

Fire alarms rang. Black, smoky water began dripping from the ceiling, flooding the floor where I lay. The echoes of modern sirens, fire alarms, and American voices bled through the weird realm of past and present we were in. Many of the spirits howled with terror when they heard the voices and noise.

"Get out of here! Now!" I pulled the salt from my pocket.

"No!" Jason struggled against Hannah, but the ghosts surged around them, pushing them both back toward the door.

Alfred removed his boot from my chest and stretched out his fingers toward the flames that engulfed the ceiling. I knew what I had to do. After the case with Lafitte, I'd made sure to memorize the Prayer of Deliverance and I didn't even need to crack open my copy of *Ghost Hunters: A Psychic's Manual* to recite it.

I sucked in what air I could, then commanded my voice to be heard over the crackling flames and wailing sirens. *"Forget the former things. Do not dwell upon the past. Your time here is over, your time among the living is done at last. Go and be judged. Go and be forgiven. Cross into the realm in which you belong."*

Several of the spirits began to flicker. Some of their faces filled with wonder. Others screamed and thrashed. One by one they disappeared, crossing over into the other place—heaven or hell or wherever the dead went. But a few, like Alfred and the three from my bedroom, still lingered, staring at me with menacing eyes. The green glow intensified around them as it died around the ghosts who had crossed.

My eyes searched out the source of the glow. From my vantage point on the floor, I could see a small, green object stuck between the bricks at the base of the cell block wall. The glow was coming from there. It must be the source of their power. Maybe it was what was keeping them here.

Voices of firefighters filled the room. Water now poured from the ceiling, drenching my smoky hair and flooding my mouth. I had to get whatever was causing the glow. Whatever it was, maybe that was the key to ending this haunting and the fires.

I crawled toward the glowing object. Alfred and the three others stepped in my way. I yanked a handful of salt from my pocket and threw it at them. They hissed and cringed when it touched their ghostly skin and recoiled.

"Alex!" A chorus of voices called my name over the din of sirens and alarm wails. Heavy footsteps clomped toward me. I swallowed painfully and lunged for the wall. I had to get it before they took me out of here.

Two firm living hands clutched me beneath the armpits and heaved me up, but not before my fingers curled around the green stone that had suddenly gone black.

Chapter Fourteen

*B*eep. *Beep. Beep. Beep.*

I awoke to the sound of a heart-rate monitor and sucked in a deep breath of antiseptic air. I knew immediately I was in the hospital.

As soon as I opened my eyes, I saw the large symbols etched in the hospital windows. Symbols that had seemed strange to me less than a year ago, but now looked so familiar. Psychics' symbols. Seals of Solomon. Ancient Egyptian and Druid symbols. Other protective sigils.

Hospitals had always taken the Problem seriously. They had to. If one malevolent ghost broke through an old ward or damaged a sigil, a dozen or more lives could be snuffed out. And now that the ghosts were running rampant in one of the New Orleans hospitals and spilling out into the city, psychic security was even more ramped up. Thankfully, I wasn't at Charity Hospital. That's the hospital where Mom and I were taken after the accident. Where Frank and Elena had been spending so much time trying to stop the spirit outbreak.

If I had to guess, I was in the New Orleans Children's Hospital. My first clue was the teen Bible and comic-like covers on the Torah and Koran at the prayer station. And this time my leg wasn't in a sling and my body didn't feel completely broken like it had after the accident. This time I felt like I'd inhaled a barbeque pit and had my head stomped on by a herd of elephants. My bones ached and the skin just below the notch where my collarbone met felt like I'd gotten a sunburn.

"You're awake." A silky, cool voice that I didn't recognize came from a chair in the darkened corner of the room.

"Yeah." My voice cracked, scraping like a blade against my parched throat. I struggled to sit up, but my pounding head pushed me back into the fluffy pillow.

A light flicked on and the figure stepped toward me. My blood froze. It was the head of OPI New Orleans, Randle Gallows. And I was alone with him.

"Where's Frank?" I asked faster than I could think.

Gallows tilted his head as if expecting me to say something else, then shrugged. "Coffee. So, before he gets back, why don't you tell me what really happened today? You don't have to hide anything from me." He said it like I was trying to hide things from Frank, but his whole demeanor changed. He came over to the bed, patted my arm, and smiled what I think he meant to be a warm smile, but came across as a grimace. "I can help you, Alex. I know Frank's busy with the hospital case; I can be there when he isn't."

A shiver wormed its way from the goose bumps in my arms to the pit of my stomach. I'd rather read Frank's entire library and become a psychic on my own than have Randle Gallows mentor me.

"Um, I think I'm supposed to debrief my mentor first." It sounded lame, but I wasn't about to tell Gallows everything that I'd seen, felt, and heard in the jail. About Alice. The prisoners. The weird green stone.

I froze. The last I could remember, the stone was clenched in my fist. It wasn't there now. I felt for my pockets, but realized I was wearing one of those breezy hospital gowns that let your butt hang out. Panic rose in my chest, making it hard to breathe. "Uh..."

He watched me carefully, a tight smile on his lips. "Come on now, tell me. What happened? What did you discover? Your report will be filed with the city OPI when it's complete, anyway."

"I—I know. But I..." I stumbled for words, feeling as though I were about to swallow a rock.

"Gallows." Frank's deep voice made me sag with relief.

"Martinez." Randle Gallows's voice went hollow. "I was just leaving."

"You shouldn't even be here. According to Section 483 of the Articles of Psychic Studies, 'students of psychic studies are required to report only to their immediate instructor or mentor. They need not report to the OPI until—'"

"I know the Articles," Gallows snapped. "I don't need them recited to me."

"Then you'll receive Alex's reports as soon as the café and Cabildo cases have been closed. *After* I've had the opportunity to review them." Frank's voice held the threat of thunder, and his eyes never left Gallows's face.

They held each other's gaze for a moment longer, then Mr. Gallows snatched up a newspaper from the chair in which he'd been sitting, and stormed from the room.

Coffee in one hand, Frank pulled a chair up beside the bed with the other and sat with a sigh. "What'd Gallows want? Details about the case, I'm guessing."

My bones still ached with cold from where the ghosts had touched me, and I wished I had a hot drink, too. Frank's eyebrows rose. "You want coffee?"

"Hot chocolate would be nice." Coffee wasn't my thing. At least not yet. It smelled okay, but the taste. Bleh. I don't know how adults could stand it.

Frank rose without a word.

"But not if you have to leave to get it," I rushed to say. I didn't want to be here alone—especially if Gallows was still lurking nearby. Frank frowned, went out the door for a moment, then came back right away.

"The nurse will get some hot cocoa brought up for you. As for Gallows, you don't need to tell him anything. He has no jurisdiction over apprentice psychics."

"But I'm not a full apprentice yet."

"Doesn't matter. You're a student. You're my student. And he has no place skulking around in here pestering you for information." Frank sat back down and took another sip of his coffee.

"He wanted to know what happened at the jail. Information about the fire cases. He said he could help me when you weren't around."

Frank stiffened at that last bit, his eyes hard. "I don't know what he's after. If anyone doesn't have time for an apprentice, it's him, not me. I suppose he thinks being *your* mentor would look good on his résumé." He gazed at the ceiling. "I'm sorry I wasn't home when you woke—"

"I was fine." I suddenly felt defensive. "I handled it."

"From what Wilhelmina said, it sounded like you needed some help closing the box."

I cringed. "So, you talked to Mrs. Wilson." Annoyance boiled my blood. Why did she have to tell Frank everything? It was like I had a spy living under my roof, not a substitute mother.

"She's not the enemy, Alex, and you know it. She only wants to help." Frank's tone was one of understanding, not blame.

"I know that." I scratched at the burning itch about an inch below the center of my collarbone.

"Don't scratch that." Frank stilled my hand with his own. "It's healing."

"What's healing?"

Frank cleared his throat. "I probably should've asked you first, but with the Sight and everything you've been going through, I thought it was in your best interest. It should help you block your mind more easily from attacks."

"Thought what was in my best interest?" I yanked at the collar of my hospital gown to find a bandage covering the area just below my collarbone.

"Here." Frank leaned forward and began carefully removing the bandage. "We can take that off now." He pulled the bandage free to reveal a new tattoo.

I didn't know whether to feel annoyed or angry or happy. It was a cool tattoo, beautiful even, but I'd never really wanted tattoos, let alone planned on having any more than the one at the base of my skull we all got at birth for protection. I sighed. As a psychic, I suppose it was something I'd have to get used to. "It's...it's cool," I managed. And the fact that a famous psychic like Frank had picked it out for me was really cool, but still.

"I'm sorry I didn't ask." Frank sat back with a huff. "But it's a sensitive spot and you were unconscious. It was a good time to have it done."

"Really. It's okay. Um, what is it?"

Frank burst out with a laugh. "Oh, Alex. Sometimes I forget that you just came into your gifts. You're so advanced in so many ways, but there's still so much for you to learn."

Yeah. Right. Like I needed reminding. "I know, but—"

"I didn't mean that in a bad way. You're more advanced than most psychics your age."

"Really?"

"Really."

"Even though I'm behind in my studies?"

Pfft. Frank scoffed, letting out a puff of air through his lips. "That's book learning. You'll catch up soon enough. You're almost there." He leaned forward, dark eyes intent. "But what you have is talent. Raw, natural talent. If we hone that properly, then you stand a good chance at really making a big difference in the world."

Me, make a big difference in the world? And here I was worried about if I'd ever become a fully Certified Apprentice Psychic. I nearly laughed I felt so giddy, now fully happy Frank had given me this new tattoo. "So, what's it mean?" I asked, glancing down at the black ink that scrolled into a hand shape on my chest with a blazing blue eye at the base of the palm.

Frank handed me a small mirror he'd found lying near the hospital sink. "It's a Hamsa, an ancient Mesopotamian symbol used to protect the wearer from the evil eye. Upright, as it is, it provides powerful protection. And since Mr. Wilkes and those prisoners tried to choke you, I thought protecting your heart and neck regions would be a good place to start."

With the mirror, I could see it properly now. Intricate scrollwork was etched in black ink around the periphery of the hand, and a black Star of David like the ones that decorated so many spirit boxes was at the base of the palm with a small cross in the center, just below a brilliant blue eye.

"Most modern religions embrace the Hamsa, which is why I made sure the OPI tattoo artist included the symbols of each. Not only will those symbols reflect and strengthen your own faith, but if ghosts of different faiths see it, it will have more power on them as well." Frank scratched his cheek. "It was meant to be a birthday gift, but I decided having you get it a few weeks early would be okay under the circumstances."

Birthday? Right, my birthday was in a couple of weeks. I was about to turn thirteen. Hannah had said something about Mrs. Wilson making dinner for me, but I'd totally forgotten about it with everything that had been happening. Alice. The prison ghosts. The fires.

The fires! How could I forget?

I sat up with a jolt, making my head throb more. "The stone," I whispered, unsure if anyone was standing outside my hospital room door. "I found a green stone at the Cabildo. Except when I saw it, the place looked like an old jail. It was this little rock, forced into a crack in the wall." I told him about the spirits I'd crossed, about the green light, and about how the malevolent prisoners had seemed to draw power from it. "It was in my hand before I blacked out." Terror tore through me. What if a firefighter had found it? Or Gallows?

"It's here." Frank reached into his pocket. "It's right here." He dropped it into my hand without question. "At first I thought nothing of it, but when you wouldn't let it go, I realized it must be important. You have a very tight grip, you know that?"

I gave him a lopsided smile and studied the bright, forest-green rock in my hand. It wasn't just a green rock. It was carved into a green skull that had been etched with tiny, intricate symbols.

"When I saw what it was, I knew it was important. I showed it to Monique when she came to check on you."

"Madame Monique was here?" I interrupted despite being insanely curious about the little skull in my hand.

Frank smiled. "Of course she was. As were Elena and Jason and Hannah and your dad. They'll be back tomorrow."

Dad had been here? Whoa. I hadn't seen him in weeks. I must've really scared everyone. But the small green skull drew my attention. "What is this?" I held up the skull to the light, which gave it an eerie green glow.

"I think it's key to the spirits and fires we've been seeing. It's called Moldavite. The stone itself has energy to bring about life transformation and spiritual awakening, which is probably why we've been seeing so many ghosts from the fire. They've likely been dormant all these years, but this stone awoke them."

"And the fires?" I asked, feeling repulsed that a single stone could give ghosts the power to wreak so much havoc.

"There haven't been any more fires since the Cabildo. Monique wants to study the symbols, but our best guess is that someone placed it there. A very alive someone."

"But who?" I asked, wondering why someone would set out a stone to purposefully stir up malevolent ghosts.

Frank shrugged. "That's yet to be seen. But Monique believes the stone has given the spirits power to seek vengeance for their deaths, and that they're the ones, with the power of the stone, that have been causing the fires in the French Quarter."

I felt sick that it was still here and not with Madame Monique. "Why didn't she take it with her?"

"We both felt it was best if you could see it when you woke up. What you saw may help decode its meaning."

"And what about the hospital haunting you and Elena have been working on? Are they related to the fires?" I was antsy to get out of the hospital and get to the bottom of what was causing all this ghost-related activity.

Frank pinched the bottom of his lip and frowned. "We're not sure yet. The OPI is looking into it. So is Elena. Of course there haven't been any fires at the hospital, but someone has eroded the wards there and that same someone must be causing the flare-up in activity. Just like someone had to put that stone in the Cabildo."

"You mean an alive someone," I said. "Someone who wants there to be more ghosts."

"Possibly. But so far we don't have any leads. As I'm sure you can imagine, Gallows is all over it, which is probably a big part of why he was here trying to get information. Once you're well enough, I need the reports on the café and the Cabildo, which means we need to set things right at the café and help Alice join her parents."

Frank was right. There was a lot of work to do. "How long have I been here? And when do I get out of this place?" I sat up and swung my legs over the edge of the bed, despite my pounding head. "I'm not doing you, Alice, or anyone else any good in here."

Frank pushed me back against the pillow. "You've been out for just over three days. It's the morning of November fourth."

"Three days?" I hated losing time. Still, I supposed three days was better than the three months I'd been in the hospital after the car accident.

"Rest for now. I'll go see about your hot chocolate. And if the doctor says your scans are okay, we'll see about getting you discharged."

Susan McCauley

Chapter Fifteen

I was totally annoyed that I had to spend another night in the hospital for one last brain scan, but the doctor couldn't find anything abnormal—despite the recent headaches—and had agreed I could be released. Besides, Madame Monique's herbs seemed to help more than the ibuprofen or whatever they were giving me in the hospital. I was eager to see what she thought about my headaches, what'd been happening to me, and what in Solomon's name was going on with the green stone I'd found.

I clenched it tight in the little sack Frank had given me, feeling the shape of the small skull inside the soft cloth. It felt heavy in my hand, dark somehow. But at least it was safe and out of the Cabildo. And there hadn't been any more fires. So that was a good thing.

Dad walked in the room with an old suitcase of mine before Frank had even woken up from his night in the hospital recliner. "The doctor said you're ready to be discharged."

"Uh, great," I said, keeping the bag with the stone concealed. I had no idea Dad would be here today. And why had he brought my old suitcase? I slowly swung my legs over the bed, excited that my head wasn't currently throbbing.

Dad handed me the bag. "I brought some of your old clothes. Get changed, and we'll go home."

Home? "Uh, I live with Frank now, Dad. I mean, I'm happy to see you and I appreciate the clothes and everything, but I don't know if they'll fit... We got some new ones a couple weeks ago because I'd outgrown everything." I didn't bother telling him that Frank had already brought me an overnight bag with clothes and a toothbrush, but I unzipped the small suitcase Dad had handed me anyway. I didn't want to hurt his feelings.

"You need to rest. The doctor told me about your headaches." He scratched his clean-shaven chin. "He said that they didn't just start. I know you're in training to be a psychic and that we're supposed to treat it like boarding school, but that doesn't mean I stopped being your father. I want you to come home until we can get you feeling better."

"The only way that will happen is if he stays with me." Frank was wide awake now and standing behind my dad. He could be stealthy when he wanted; I hadn't even heard him get up.

"You haven't even told me how his studies are going," Dad turned on Frank and snapped.

"You haven't asked," Frank snapped back. Frank was a foot taller than Dad with broader shoulders and crazy tattoos, especially the gargoyle tattoo that looked like it might fly off Frank's forearm and attack.

Then there was Dad. Balding and pale and kinda short. He could be feisty when he wanted to be, but my mom had been the fierce one. She'd been a lot like Frank. Dad could stand his ground, but I knew he didn't stand a chance about getting his way. Not with this.

I didn't want him to.

I wanted to go back to the apartment. It wasn't just Frank's place; it was mine, too. I didn't have any sad reminders of Mom there, and everything in my life now was at the apartment, especially all things psychic: spirit traps, ghost books, psychic wards, escrima sticks, holy water, salt, protective herbs, Mrs. Wilson, Madame Monique. My old home just reminded me of everything I'd lost.

"I love you, Dad," I said, yanking on the jeans he'd brought, which were two inches too short and ultra-tight in the crotch. "But I need to go back with Frank."

"But..." Dad sputtered.

"Really," I said, pulling the old ghostball team T-shirt over my head. Thankfully, that still fit. "I need to learn to control my abilities. That's the key to getting the headaches to stop. And between Frank and Madame Monique, I know we can do it."

Dad lowered his gaze, his eyes glistening. "Are you sure?"

"Yes."

Hands on my shoulders, he searched my face. "Are you sure you're okay? I...I've missed you."

I reached out and gave him an awkward hug. "I've missed you, too. But I'm sure Elena's told you I'm okay, hasn't she?" I mean, Aunt Elena was Dad's sister. And she and Hannah still did live next door to Dad. It wasn't like he was completely cut off from me and my new life.

"She has," Dad said. "I just— If you need anything, you'll let me know?"

"Of course I will." I gave his shoulders one last squeeze and let go.

Dad swallowed and took back the suitcase he'd handed me. "You're right," he said, looking me up and down. "You have grown."

Frank opened his mouth, likely to remind me he'd brought clothes that actually fit me, but I gave him a tiny shake of my head. "Yeah. But they're good enough to get me home."

"Home?" A mix of fear and eagerness filled his eyes.

"Uh, yeah. Frank's place." I guess the apartment really was my home.

"Oh, right." His shoulders slumped for a moment, but then he straightened and smiled. "I'm very proud of you, Alex. I know you've been through a lot the past several months. We both have. But you even more than me. I know I didn't make it easy at first—with my feelings about psychics—but you're doing it. You're doing what you were meant to. Your mom would be proud, too."

"Thanks," I said, willing my tears not to come. "I know she would be."

Frank had let me stuff myself with Café Du Monde beignets and freshly squeezed orange juice on the way home from the hospital since I hadn't had any decent food in days. It'd been a bit of a pain for Frank to find a parking spot in his large, heavily warded, pre-owned OPI white van, but he didn't seem to mind the trouble. He even ate a plate of beignets himself.

Our stomachs full, we climbed into the van for the short ride back to the apartment. I hardly ever rode in Frank's van since I'd been with him; he was always driving it to and from the hospital, and my cases had been walkable in the French Quarter. That was fine by me. I liked to walk. But his van was kind of cool in a freakish, psychic kind of way.

Wards and seals were scrawled all over the outside of the van in iron ward paint. There were nearly invisible symbols etched into the windows, and the inside glowed with extra seals of protection. In the back, there was a fully equipped psychic investigator/paranormal investigator setup. Frank and Elena had made modifications to the usual vans the OPI psychics used and created space for EVP playback, a screen for watching video and infrared footage, and had some other cool gadgets set up that I hadn't yet asked about. Of course, there was also a small arsenal of psychic tools, too: iron ward paint, blessed Red Sea salt, holy water, sage, and iron-tipped escrima sticks. It was like an enhanced mini-OPI office on wheels with added paranormal investigation tools.

My thoughts left the gear and gadgets as we rounded the corner onto Royal Street. When I saw Solomon's Eye and our apartment building, my heart sagged with relief. It was good to be home. I leapt out before Frank even finished parking, and as soon as I walked through the front door of the apartment, Onyx gave a loud meow and jumped into my arms. Mrs. Wilson was there blubbering and pulled me into a fierce hug.

And to my surprise, their touch didn't hurt. Not at all. In fact, they didn't feel as cold as they used to. Onyx even felt soft and not really warm, but not cold either.

I hugged Mrs. Wilson back, managing to keep my arms from sliding through her, which was getting easier with practice. Onyx wasn't so hard to touch because he was a solid apparition. Mrs. Wilson was trickier since she was a visible apparition and somewhat transparent. It seemed like how transparent they were or weren't had been definitely linked with how solid they felt when I touched them.

"You're hugging Wilhelmina." Frank came in behind me, my forgotten overnight bag in his hand.

"Yeah, I am." I patted her shoulder as she continued to blubber. "I'm sorry I got so mad at you, Mrs. Wilson. I really am...I shouldn't have—"

"Don't even worry about that." She flapped a pudgy hand in the air, then pulled me back into a weeping hug. "Frank told me what happened when he came to get your bag. Those *evil* ghosts touched you." She gritted her teeth, then her whole body quivered. "And you went to the hospital. I thought I'd lost you forever!" she bawled.

"It's okay. I'm okay. Really. I feel better than I did before," I said with an uncertain shrug.

"It's the Hamsa tattoo. I noticed how much better I felt when they touched me after I got mine." He pulled the neck of his shirt collar down low to reveal his own hand-shaped tattoo, which was inked just below an intricate Fourth Pentacle of the Moon tattoo. "I had the artist place a Fourth Pentacle of the Moon inside your Hamsa. I would've done the same thing with mine, but I already had this one," he said, pointing at the black Fourth Pentacle of the Moon just below the notch in his sternum, "before I ever knew how powerful—and helpful—the Hamsa could be."

Gratitude rolled over me. Even if getting tattoos hadn't been high on my to-do list, I sure was glad I had this one. I wouldn't have to worry about taking it off or leaving it on at night like I did with my Nazar Boncuğu. This one was powerful and permanent protection. "Thanks again, Frank. Really." Onyx purred and rubbed up against me, making me feel all loved and tingly instead of weak and cold.

"You're welcome. It's the least I could do for your thirteenth birthday."

"Your birthday?" Mrs. Wilson gasped. "I didn't miss your birthday, did I? Oh no!" She sunk her head in her hands, shoulders shaking with renewed sobs. She was so dramatic it was almost funny, except that she was upset.

"No, Wilhelmina, you didn't miss it." Frank gave her a consoling rub on what he could touch of her back.

"It's on December first. Plenty of time before my birthday."

"Right," she said with a sniff, straightening herself. "Then I still have time to plan a little party for you."

"But we don't have birthday parties. Not after we turn ten." I didn't want to hurt her feelings, but that's the way it was. Ten was the magic number when kids—well, kids except for me—found out if they were psychic or not. Ten was the last year for birthday parties, unless you were Hannah, of course. She planned on having birthday parties forever.

"Nonsense," Mrs. Wilson tutted, wiping away a phantom tear. "A little dinner party never hurt anybody." And with that she floated toward the kitchen, humming.

"If it makes her happy, let her do it." Frank fondly watched her round backside disappear through the wall.

I shrugged. "Hannah wanted to do something, anyway. So, I guess if it's just a dinner party, it'll be okay."

Just as the words left my lips, Hannah, Jason, Elena, and Madame Monique tromped into the apartment.

Hannah wore her usual determined expression and carried an iron spirit trap in one hand and her PI investigation kit in the other. Jason followed close behind with a bulging duffle bag slung over one shoulder and a plate of fried plantains in his other hand. "I've got more collapsible escrima sticks." He grinned and pulled a fried plantain from the plate with his teeth, chomping down on it as he talked. "One for everybody." He held the plate up for me to take. "And these are from Mom. She says you need to eat to gain your strength. She also knows they're your favorite." He swiped another fried sweet plantain and popped it in his mouth.

"Hey!" I cradled the plate protectively to my chest with a smile. "Leave some for me." They were Jason's favorites, too. But Jason knew I'd share anything with him, especially food.

Elena followed Jason inside with a large sack that she promptly took into the living room and began to unload. "I've brought everything we need to end this, once and for all. Blessed salt from the Red Sea, holy water, sage," she called over her shoulder as she set the bags and bottles on Frank's desk.

Madame Monique brought up the rear of the bizarre parade, carrying only a tiny glass bottle with a small, mysterious smile on her face.

They surrounded me with chatter, not giving me a moment to speak until we were all settled in the living room, which also served as Frank's office and my training area. Jason and Hannah sat on either side of me. Frank leaned up against his desk. Elena was in my usual chair, and Madam Monique stood in the center of the room facing me.

"I saw the stone while you were unconscious," Madame Monique announced, her voice heavy with knowledge. "But I must study it more closely if my knowledge is to be of use."

I squirmed under her gaze, then shoved my hand in my pocket and retrieved the little green skull. Palm open, I raised it toward her for all to see.

Madame Monique stepped closer, her eyes never leaving mine. "May I take it? Only for a moment?"

I nodded, feeling suddenly lighter once the skull left my fingers. "You can keep it for as long as you want," I said, not sure if I even wanted it back. Something felt off about it.

"*Merci.*" She seemed to speak French when she was particularly focused on something. Then, taking the stone in her hand, she popped a jeweler's loupe in one eye and inspected the skull closely.

No one said a word. There was no sound. No motion. Nothing except the ticking swing of the pendulum on the hall clock. *Tok, tic, tok, tic.* It swung back and forth and back and forth. A metronome of drowsy waiting.

Madame Monique turned the miniature skull over and over in her hand, inspecting every angle. Finally, she popped the jeweler's loupe out of her eye socket and sighed. "It is as I suspected." She turned to Frank then back to me, her Haitian accent heavier than usual. "I am certain it is Moldavite, which is a vitreous silica formed by a meteorite impact in Europe that occurred about fifteen million years ago. It is not too rare, but it is a very powerful stone." Madame Monique held the stone up for all of us to see. "Rich forest green. A beautiful specimen. Powerful. But carved like a skull with many ancient symbols. This was designed to cause harm."

"Has it been causing all the fires and spirit activity in the Quarter?" I asked the question I'd been burning to learn the answer to since Frank had given the stone back to me in the hospital.

"On its own, no. But in the hands of someone who plays with dark magic. *Oui*." She nodded, her brown eyes troubled. "It could disturb the spirits, give them power so they could cause the fires." She ran her finger gently over the tiny markings. "These are ancient symbols. To cause fires. To raise ghosts. To create destruction." She shook her head. "This stone was intended for evil." She walked over to me and placed the stone back in my palm.

My fingers tingled, and my hand felt heavy. I didn't want this burden. "What am I supposed to do with it?" I offered it back to her.

She gave me a tiny shake of the head and curled my fingers around it. "Go back to where it all began. Back to the place where the fires started. Use the stone to draw the spirits to you."

"But how?" What was I supposed to do, stand there and call them? I didn't even know how many there were. There was Alice and the one prisoner, Alfred. But there were also three other nameless convict spirits roaming around out there—and maybe more.

Madame Monique pulled a folded piece of parchment from her pocket and handed it to me. "I've consulted my books. I believe this will work to help you call them. Use it together with the stone. Then, God willing, you can cross them over."

CHAPTER SIXTEEN

The fire of 1788 had originally started at the home of Don Vicente Jose Nunez, paymaster of the army, right next door to the place Alice had lived—and died. So, we'd done what Madame Monique had suggested and gone back to where we'd started the investigation: the burnt-out café. Nunez's old home.

If there was any chance of putting the three criminal ghosts and Alice to rest, it was now. I hadn't seen Alice since the fire at the prison. Maybe she was afraid I'd be angry at her for taking me into a fiery jail full of malevolent spirits. Or maybe she was just hiding from the other ghosts.

Frank and Elena were inside setting up a table with gear. Several battery-operated lanterns had already been set throughout the building, filling the carcass of the café with weary light. Still, it was more than I'd had last time. Even Frank, who disliked using electricity, had agreed we needed more light than headlamps for this job, and batteries were safer than plugging in work lights.

Hannah had given everyone extra salt and holy water for the job.

"She almost wiped out my personal supply." Elena laughed. "I'm glad I put an order in yesterday."

"Well, we never know how much we'll need," she said, in response to Frank's amused expression.

And, true to his word, Jason had given each member of our team collapsible, iron-tipped escrima sticks.

In addition to Hannah's extra precautions, Madame Monique had made sure we were all wearing our Nazar Boncuğus and had insisted we all drink shots of her special Green Ghost before leaving for the job.

"If they come at you," Jason said, extending the escrima stick with a click of a button and flip of the wrist so that the stick fully extended. "Just poke 'em like this!" He jabbed it into the air, his shadow making him look like a sword-wielding pirate.

"Got it," Hannah said, securing the stick in a pocket not bulging with salt and bottles of holy water.

"Good." Jason nodded, collapsed his stick and tucked it into his own pocket, before going to the gear table to remove his *specula spiritis* and Spirit Horn from their cases. He secured the ghost glasses on his head and looked about the husk of the café. "Nothing here yet," he announced.

"Nope. Not yet," I said.

"I really need a pair of those things," Hannah said, testing the battery on her EVP recorder. "Elena can sense them. Frank and Alex can see and hear them. And now you can see them with those goggles and hear them with that horn, but what about me?"

Elena set down the EMF detector she'd just filled with new, specially warded batteries, and went over to Hannah. "You should know something is here with the EMF detector. That's why I use PI equipment. It's why I became a paranormal investigator. My abilities aren't very strong at all. I could mistake a ghost for the wind." It was true. As a Class C Psychic, Aunt Elena didn't have very reliable abilities. She could sense things, but it was nothing like what Frank and I could feel and see as Class A Psychics.

"I know that," Hannah admitted quietly. "But I don't have any abilities at all."

It was time I said something. I was tired of Hannah seeming to think she was less than us. Less than me. She totally wasn't. Not at all. When I walked over to them, Elena smiled and took a step back.

"Hannah, you do have abilities," I said. "Lots of them. You're wicked smart with all things paranormal. You know how to use *all* of this gear." I gestured to the array of gadgets on the table with Madame Monique's herbs and charms scattered over it. "You understand what to look and listen for with EMF and EVP readings. You captured proof that one of the entities was set on burning things. You're freakin' amazing," I told her, and before I knew it she'd thrown her arms around me in a big, teary hug.

Grinning, Elena put her arms around us both. "And, most important," she lifted Hannah's chin, "you understand the extent of the Problem. You know how and why we can and should work with psychics to help spirits cross over. There are more ghosts trapped here than there are psychics to deal with them. So, if we can get more Class C Psychics and Untouched to help us with the Problem, the fewer malevolent spirits we'll have wreaking havoc on the living. Right?"

Hannah's lips quivered into a smile, some of her usual confidence flooding back into her. "Right."

"We're a team," I smiled, and escaped the awkward group hug with a mix of relief and happiness. "So, let's get on with sending *these* spirits wherever they need to go."

Hannah nodded, her confidence back in place. "Yes. Let's do this."

Elena turned back to the table to finish checking that all the gear was fully charged and in top working order, and Hannah gently tugged my arm. "Are you ready, Alex?" she asked so softly no one else could hear.

My throat was still raw from the smoke, my skin still burned from the new tattoo, I had a slight pounding in my head since I'd been touched by so many spirits, and I was afraid of what those murderous ghosts might do if they got their hands around my throat again...but what choice did I have? If I didn't cross them over, I'd never become a fully Certified Apprentice Psychic. And I'd have Alice and a bunch of eighteenth-century fugitives popping up scaring me for the rest of my life. "Yeah. I'm ready."

"We've got your back, X." Jason walked up to us, grinning like a mad scientist with the ghost glasses magnifying one eye and Spirit Horn in hand. He looked crazy, but I didn't laugh this time. I guess I was getting used to it.

"I know you do, J." I smiled. "You, too, Hannah. I'm glad you're both here."

"Of course we're here. Like you said. We're a team." Hannah clipped the EVP recorder to her belt and flipped on her EMF detector.

"And Hannah," Jason added, "I'll talk to Madame Monique. It's taken her years to get these to work," he gestured at the *specula spiritis.* "But maybe we can come up with something to help you see them, too."

Hannah's smile broke into a full-on grin. "That would be awesome. In the meantime, I'm going to do my best to capture another awesome EVP."

"Great," I said, not feeling ready to call the ghosts back with the skull, fearing what the Sight might show me. "No time like the present." Frank was just painting the final touches on some iron wards he'd added to the windows, and I knew he'd be ready.

"Everybody grab a bag of salt." Elena directed us to the extra sacks she had stacked on the table. "While Frank's finishing the wards, we're going to line the perimeter with salt. Alex, you take that wall. Hannah, that one. Jason, that one." She pointed me to the back and Hannah and Jason to the side walls. "Maybe it's a good thing we brought extra." Elena gave Hannah an encouraging smile. "I'll get the front wall. Then we'll go to the kitchen and get that room, too."

"Make sure you don't miss the windowsills and doorways," Frank said, adding an additional iron-paint ward to a small window. "And Alex, after you set out the stone and call the spirits with the incantation Madame Monique gave you, I'll put the final ward on the door. Once they're here, they'll be trapped. There'll be no way out unless they cross over. If things go bad, we can use the spirit traps Jason brought, and then cross them one at a time." Frank pointed to the bulging duffle bag on the table.

I'd been wondering what was in there, so I went over and peeked inside.

"Primed ghostballs." Jason grinned. "Frank couldn't get any proper spirit traps from the OPI, and the iron spirit box was damaged from the fall."

"All in use at the hospital," Frank grumbled.

"So, I figured since they worked on Mr. Wilkes, they will work in a pinch here, too."

"Great thinking, J!" I smiled, inspecting the ward work on the balls. "And you painted the seals?"

Jason shrugged modestly. "Madame Monique's been making me practice."

"Good woman," Frank grunted, his eyes fixed intently on a symbol he was painting to ward a final pane of glass.

"You need to know how to paint them, draw them, create them with your eyes closed. Especially if you're going to be hanging around with this lot."

I snorted back a laugh. Never in a trillion years had I thought Jason and I would end up in a haunted house hunting ghosts together.

"Salt," Elena called out. "Let's get it down and get started. The sun's just set, but it'd be nice to wrap up before midnight."

We'd decided to wait until sunset to call the spirits since they were typically the most active at night, but that also meant they could be more powerful. There wasn't any conclusive research on it yet, but it seemed they were at the height of their strength at the darkest hours of the night, and that their strength and visibility waned in the sunlight. That didn't mean there were no ghosts during the day; there were plenty. It just meant we had a better chance of everybody turning up at night.

After covering the perimeter of the café with salt, including the burnt-out bathroom and storeroom, all the windowsills and doorways, with extra over the front threshold, we were finally ready.

We stood in the area where Alice had been when she died—trapped beneath that solid oak table. Now it was only a gray and blackened space, the table long destroyed. But I knew I would soon be taken back to her world of smoke and flames and death.

Frank and Elena hovered just on the other side of the swinging kitchen door to monitor any activity in the front room. They were only steps away and would come to us if the ghosts appeared here first. Beside me, a few feet away, Jason wore his *specula spiritis*, the Spirit Horn held up to his ear. Hannah was a few feet from me on the other side, her EVP recorder switched on, EMF detector at the ready.

"Right," I said, exhaling a deep breath. "Let's do this." I didn't feel brave or courageous as I took the small pouch with the skull from my pocket, together with the parchment Madame Monique had given me. I felt small and unsure. But, come what may, I had to do what needed to be done. That was part of being psychic. I set the stone carving on the floor in front of me and unfolded the parchment.

I squatted beside the stone so I could read the paper in a stream of lantern light.

"The heart of the dead man is weighed in the scales of the balance against the feather of righteousness. O, my heart, which I had from my mother!" My voice broke the silence and my heart twisted painfully at that line. A line from an ancient Egyptian text that Madame Monique said was important. Important because it made the text all the more personal to me, all the more powerful. Mom was with me. Even though she was dead. Even though she had crossed over, she was part of me. Part of my skin and blood and bones. She loved me. And that love held power. And that power would help me do what I was meant to do. I cleared my throat and continued, louder and clear than before:

"O, my heart, which I had from my mother! O, my heart of different ages! Do not stand against me, spirits, do not be opposed to me, do not be hostile to me in the presence of the Keeper of the Balance. Come to me now! Come, so you may go forth to the happy place whereto we speed."

The last word died on my lips, and all was quiet.

Silence. Darkness. Smoke.

Stillness filled the air, only minute motes of dust and ash swirled and danced between the seams of shadow and light.

Jason shifted on his feet. Hannah hissed at him to hush. Nothing.

I waited, trying to be patient. What if this didn't work?

Then the lanterns flickered, and the small skull of Moldavite began to glow. Soft at first, but growing brighter and deeper green each second until the lantern light was swallowed up completely.

The temperature in the room dropped and the feeling of icy fire coursed over my skin. Hannah let out a deep breath, exhaling a great plume of mist into the stale, green air.

"It's getting cold. Fast." She zipped up the hoodie she was wearing, eyes huge behind her thick-framed glasses, then held up her EMF detector. The lights weren't blinking like crazy yet, but it was only a matter of time.

Jason's magnified eye scanned the room. "See anything yet, X?"

"Not yet. But they're coming. I can feel them."

The light from the Moldavite was so bright I couldn't see the skull itself, but it pulsated now, dull and throbbing, like some sort of beacon for the dead.

A cold tingle, like the trailing of a finger along my right arm, shot shivers along my skin and down my spine. Then a voice drifted up beside me.

"I'm here." Alice. Her voice barely more than a whisper. "I'm—I'm sorry about what happened at the jail. Please don't be angry with me. But you had to see. I had to show you the stone. It's how they're making the fires. And it makes me mean."

"I know." I beckoned her to come closer. She emerged from the shadowy corner. I looked beyond her burnt face and clothes to see a frightened little girl. "You were just trying to help. You were very brave."

She shuffled her feet through ash and charred rubble as she approached.

"Are you hurt?" She held my hand, turning it back and forth in her own. "Did the mean one hurt you?"

"Yes." I wasn't going to lie. Alice had led me into a very dangerous situation. I could have died. But I didn't. And now I had the Hamsa for extra protection. "But I'm okay now."

"Good." She gave me a teary smile and dropped my hand. "You feel different."

I smiled back. "So do you." She wasn't painfully cold anymore. We weren't in the past yet. She was a ghost girl in front of me, and her touch didn't hurt.

Suddenly, Alice jerked her head around as if she heard a noise and the green light strobed brighter, then faded to a constant glow. "They're coming now. The last of them are coming."

She pulled away from me and went to her hiding place beneath the oak table. And just like that, I was back in the past.

Smoke clung to the air, and flames lapped at the walls. Again, we were reliving the moment of Alice's death. I could see the faint outlines of Jason and Hannah, as if they were barely visible ghosts in this weird plane of the past. I heard their voices, distant and echoey.

"It'll be different this time," I told Alice, reaching inside myself to find the courage that felt as if it were leaking from me in a giant spaghetti strainer. "Don't look at the bad men, just look for the light. When you see it, go to it, okay? Your parents are there. Try not to be afraid. Just go to the light."

"Uh-uh." She shook her head and scooted farther into the shadows, just as she had for her father.

She wasn't going to make this easy, was she? But I supposed ghosts never did. If it were easy, nobody would really need psychics. I sighed. "Right. Then, just stay behind me." I would deal with the prisoner ghosts, then, maybe, I could finally help Alice be at peace.

Four translucent figures shrouded in smoke and flames appeared before me, their crooked bodies silhouetted against the green glow of the skull. The outlines of manacles still appeared on their ankles, but the chains had melted away, the scent of molten metal and burning hair and skin ripe in the smoky air.

The largest of the phantoms, whom I recognized as Alfred, the ghost who'd escaped me at home and then nearly crushed my chest at the prison, stood in front of the other three. They leered at me, rage and power filling their spiteful eyes.

"You moved the source of our power, boy," Alfred snarled. "But no matter now, I suppose." He shrugged and lifted his foot, now free of the ball and chain to which he'd been tethered. "It's freed us already, and we will take what energy we can from it, then be gone from this place. We will have our revenge on the people of this city."

"No one in this city caused you harm. They're all dead. They died years ago. I know you had a terrible death, and I'm sorry. No one deserves—"

"You're right," snapped one of the prisoners from behind Alfred. "No one deserves to be thrown in jail for stealing meat to feed his starving family, and then be chained up and forgotten in a rotten, smelly hole and burned alive. No one deserves that! But that was my fate. And the people of the city *will* pay!"

Another of the prisoners rumbled his agreement. "I, too, was jailed for stealing. Was it such a crime that I should have been left to burn alive? Even Alfred here," he motioned toward the leader. "He was imprisoned for murder and set to be hanged. But the fire came. And he, along with us, was left chained and forgotten and burned alive. Is that a fit punishment?"

Alfred was a murderer. I didn't know the circumstances and dared not ask. Would it make a difference if he'd murdered in self-defense or out of anger? Perhaps. Perhaps not. But by the look of him, he'd led a rough life. Still, it was not my place to judge. God would do that. It was my place to help him cross over. And now I understood that each of these ghosts needed to tell their story. If they did, then maybe I could find a way to help put them at ease. Help them find a way to peace within themselves and go where they belonged.

The last of the four prisoners was quiet and thin and held himself back. His head hung low, and I could barely see his eyes for the wild mane of unkempt hair that partially covered his face. "And what about you?" I asked, focusing my energy on the man. "Why were you in prison?"

There was a moment of silence. The others stirred, but did not respond. I took a bold step forward, the cold reeling off of the spirits intensifying, making me extra glad for the Hamsa tattoo. "I'm sorry. I don't know your name, but I'd like to know. Why were you in prison?"

One of the others nudged the quiet man, as if they were boys who'd been caught and sent to the principal's office. The thin ghost stepped forward, his eyes lonely and sad and hollow. "I—"

"Tell 'im, Gaspar. Tell 'im how unfair it is. Tell 'im why you're here. Why we're here. Why we'll not leave until we've had our vengeance." Alfred's voice held the threatening promise of pain.

The thin ghost, Gaspar, gave a long, mournful sigh. "I committed no crime." His eyes met mine and in an instant I could see the clear honesty of his words. "I was falsely accused of stealing guns from the arsenal. I was simply in the wrong place at the wrong time." He shrugged. "Apparently I looked like the thief, and it didn't matter that they could find no guns or ammunition on my person. Nothing at all."

"Then why are you still here?" I gaped at him.

Rage flickered in his gaze. "My wife was about to give birth. I was on my way to fetch the midwife when they took me. I never got to see my child. They told me I had a daughter. Her name was Anna. My wife was going to fight for me. Fight to make them release me... Fight so I could hold my baby girl." Tears glistened in his eyes. "But then the fire came." He choked back a sob. "I don't even know if my little girl survived the fire. She or my wife."

It felt as if eels squirmed around my heart, slimy and wet and horrendous. To die such a death and not know the fate of your family. I could hardly begin to imagine the pain.

Four men. Each with a story. One a murderer. Two thieves. One innocent. All trapped in a dirty jail and burned alive with no chance of escape. It was a horrible death. Something no one deserved.

"What happened to you wasn't fair." Alfred stirred, but I kept talking. "Not to any of you. Everyone deserves a trial. Deserves a chance at proving his innocence." I sighed. I had to help them put their need for vengeance to rest. They had to cross over and stop hurting the living. "It isn't my place to judge you. I'm here to help you move on. You don't belong here anymore."

"I want my vengeance!" Alfred's words bit the air, but the other three seemed less sure now.

"Vengeance on who? On what? The people who imprisoned you—the people who left you in the fire—are long dead. You've already caused fires that have taken the lives of innocent people. Is that fair?"

I tried to understand the pain and anger. I wanted to understand. "Is it fair to take those people from their husbands and wives, from their mothers and fathers, from their own children?" My voice caught in my throat at the pang of losing my own mother. "It's time to move on. Put the past to rest and have peace. Go and join your loved ones."

Gaspar's eyes shined with fresh tears. "I just want to see my wife and daughter."

"And you will." I smiled at him. "It's been hundreds of years since the fire, sir. They would have moved on by now. Just like it's time for you to move on."

"I want to see my sister," said another, the rage now drained from his face.

"It's been hundreds of years?" the third prisoner asked.

I nodded. "Yes, sir. Well over two hundred years."

His mouth gaped in wonder and he shook his head. "It...it doesn't seem possible."

Time moved differently for ghosts; I'd learned that much. They could get stuck in loops replaying their deaths over and over again, or sometimes they were so caught up in feelings of anger or revenge they lost all sense of time.

The green glow of the Moldavite skull pulsed weakly, as if the spirits' fading anger was draining away its power.

Only Alfred still scowled, but now he had removed himself from the others, his fists clenched. I'd better help the three willing ghosts cross now, before Alfred lost his temper.

I spoke the words of the crossing prayer I'd learned for Mrs. Wilkes, which felt like a really long time ago. *"No matter what you've done or what you fear, spirit, your place to stay is no longer here. Your life and time is now complete. Move into the light that shines before you, then in time you'll be cleansed."*

Alfred screamed and the Moldavite skull flared bright green, but he was too late. The other three ghosts were transfixed by a beautiful white and golden light that shined from the farthest corner of the room.

Gaspar's eyes shined bright and sparkling, and his mouth gaped open. The others gazed at him, their own faces filled with awe and wonder. "What do you see, Gaspar?"

"My wife...my daughter? My baby, Anna." Gaspar stepped forward, arms outstretched. His form began to shimmer and fade, mixing with the light.

"Our time here is not through! We must seek vengeance!" Alfred yelled, shielding his eyes from the pure, white light.

The two thieves shook their heads at him, all rage gone. "Whatever our fate, it is time to meet it. This boy is right. Our place is no longer here."

They turned their backs on Alfred and stepped into the light. Alfred roared with rage as it swirled around them, combining with their essences and absorbing them, transporting them to another place. A place I could only imagine. I wondered if they would still have to pay for their crimes, or if their suffering here on earth had been payment enough.

I turned back to Alfred. "Please. It's time for you to go, too."

"No!" Alfred lunged at me.

I dodged right.

He lunged again, and the green light grew more fierce. "I don't need them. I'll take vengeance on my own." His voice held the growl of a feral dog I'd once seen on a hike with Mom, wild and ready to bite.

If he didn't want to cross, I would need to trap him. But in this strange in-between place where I could see the ghosts' pasts, I couldn't see everything in the present. I prayed Jason and Hannah could see me. Prayed that with the Spirit Horn, Jason could hear what was happening. "Ghostball!" I yelled, hoping I'd be heard. "We may need a ghostball!"

Like an echo from a distant shore I heard a voice, so faint and far away it could have been a dream. "Ghostball. Got it, X."

I hoped I was really hearing Jason. Hoped he and Hannah were able to set the trap. Hoped that Alfred didn't know what we were talking about.

After the incident with Mr. Wilkes, Frank had made me memorize King Solomon's ward of drawing and protection. I quickly drew the necessary symbols on the ground to help keep Alfred in the room with us—and the ghost trap—then hoping Jason and Hannah were ready, I began to recite the verse:

By the light

On this night

I call to Thee

To give me Your might

By the power of three

I call to thee,

Into this ghostball, Alfred.

Lord protect all

That surround me

So may it be

So may it be.

As the final words left my lips, I heard a high-pitched, terrified scream. Jerking my head to the left, I saw Alfred. He had Alice. He'd ripped her out from beneath the table, his hands tight around her tiny, pale throat. He gave me an evil grin, just as he and Alice were sucked into the ghost trap.

Susan McCauley

Chapter Seventeen

The world cleared of smoke and flames and green light nearly as quickly as it had overtaken me.

Hannah's voice drifted into my clouded brain. "Thankfully, Jason could hear some of what was going on. Otherwise we'd never have known to get the ghostball and set the trap."

I shook my head and steadied myself against the charred wall. "I'm really glad you did, but we have to let him out."

"What? Why?" Hannah gasped.

I ran my hands through my hair. "He's got Alice."

"How?" Frank's voice rumbled. "Ghost traps are only good to hold one ghost."

"Ghostballs can hold poltergeists. For the game anyway," I said. "Maybe that's why."

Jason held the ball away as if it might bite.

Frank took the ball from Jason and settled it securely in the crook of his arm. "No more ghostball traps, then. Got it?"

"But—" Jason frowned, eyes downcast.

"I know they work in a pinch. I see that. But now we've got a malevolent spirit in there with a child. That shouldn't have happened. It should never happen."

"But ghosts can't kill each other." Hannah put a consoling arm around Jason's shoulder. "And he was trying to help Alex."

"He was." Voice soft, Frank nodded his head in agreement. "And I don't blame you at all, Jason. Ghostballs are untested. A brilliant invention, for sure. But unstable—as we saw with Mr. Wilkes. Now this." He turned to Hannah. "And while ghosts can't kill each other, they can *harm* each other."

I felt the blood drain from my limbs and my head buzzed, remembering how the school janitor's spirit had been injured when he'd protected me from Mr. Wilkes. "But they recover," I said, feeling both terrified for Alice and protective of Jason. He had only been trying to help me, and I was the one who'd called for the ghost trap in the first place.

"Their essences can recover, true. But the trauma can be too much for some. And as we've seen with Alice, she's already a terrified little thing." Frank leveled his gaze at me. "So if you want to get through to her, if you want her to cross over, we need to get her out of that ball before Alfred does irreparable harm to what's left of her mind."

A sick, sinking sensation slithered into my gut, making me want to puke. "We have to get her out." I reached for the ghostball, but Frank stopped me.

"First, we need a plan of how we'll handle Alfred when he gets out." Frank waited, and all eyes rested on me. "Think, Alex. You're almost a full apprentice. What should we do? If I weren't here, what would you do?"

I tallied our gear in my head, thinking of their uses—ultra glad Hannah had insisted they bring more salt. "Let's add more protection. Here," I said, pointing to the place where I'd drawn Solomon's symbols on the ground. "Let's put a salt circle around the symbols. If he's trapped close to the symbols needed to help him cross, maybe they'll be more powerful."

Frank nodded approval and Elena, Hannah, and Jason went to the front room to get the salt.

"And I'm going to see if I caught anything on my new EVP recorder," Hannah called over her shoulder.

"Bring the holy water, too," I said. "Just in case there's more ghost fire."

"Good. What else?" Frank asked.

I spied the softly glowing Moldavite skull I'd used to conjure Alfred and the other spirits. I had an idea.

The ghostball jittered and jerked in Frank's hands, the glowing wards sparking. "Hurry with the salt! I don't think it will hold much longer." His voice bellowed through the empty shell of the building.

Elena and the others quickly returned, each carrying a large bag of salt.

Out of breath, eyes lit with excitement, Hannah hollered, "You guys have got to hear this," as she plopped down the salt bag then held up the EVP recorder. "Shhh. Now, listen." She pressed play. Static. My voice. Frank's. Jason's. "Here," she said in a whisper. More static. Then a man's voice. Deep and angry and disturbing. "*Brûlez-les, brûlez-les tous!*"

She pressed the stop button. "It's the clearest EVP I've ever caught. I can't wait to put it on Elena's system at the shop and clean it up even more."

"It is super clear, but what does it mean?" Jason asked, his one bug eye looking curiously at Hannah.

"Well done, Hannah," Elena said. "This is proof that Untouched can hear them, too. Play it again."

Hannah pressed one button, then another. Again we heard our voices, then static. Then, "*Brûlez-les, brûlez-les tous!*"

"It's definitely French." Frank leaned forward. "Not modern. Sounds like the same voice we heard before."

"Is he talking about *crème brûlée*?" Jason asked and licked his lips.

"Jason, seriously?" Hannah gasped. "How can you think of food at a time like this?"

He shrugged. "I'm always thinking of food."

I normally would have laughed, but even Jason's appetite couldn't stop the horrible feeling seeping over me as the old French started making sense in my brain—just like it did when I was in a ghost memory and could understand them. "Play it again, please. One more time."

She did. "*Brûlez-les, brûlez-les tous!*"

Frank's eyes met mine. "You know what it means?"

I swallowed, nodded. "Burn them. Burn them all."

Frank was all action after that, barking orders like he was the head of OPI. "Keep that recording, Hannah. It's a breakthrough in EVPs. The OPI will want it."

Hannah turned toward us, her cheeks glowing. "I can't believe it! The famous Frank Martinez thinks I captured a breakthrough EVP!" she whispered excitedly to me and Jason as if Frank were some sort of psychic celebrity and not our friend.

Jason and I flashed a thumbs-up at her. I was glad she'd captured something useful, even if it was a threatening message from a malevolent ghost.

"Kids, Elena. Get the salt. There's no time to waste. Let's go, now," Frank said, then went into a huddle with Elena.

Jason and I each took a bag of salt, and together we all created a large circle around the symbols I'd traced in the ash. It was large enough for three or four adults to stand in close together, and I hoped it would give Alice enough room to keep away from Alfred as we worked.

The ball sparked again as if coughing up flames, and Frank jerked his hand away. "It's getting hot."

"The circle's ready," I said. "Set it inside. Let's get Alice out of there."

So the ball wouldn't roll out of the protective circle, Frank placed it inside a small cardboard box, which had previously held some piece of PI equipment. He then took a knife from his pocket and quickly scraped away part of the iron ward paint that held the ghosts inside. The ball shook as if an earthquake had taken hold of it, and I was so glad Frank had thought to set it inside of something. It jerked and jittered and sparked, then fire shot from the ball, engulfing it in flames. The plastic smoked and melted. Was I back in some weird ghost memory or was I still with my friends?

They were all there beside me. I was in the present, and the salt circle held.

Putrid, black smoke rose into the air as the ball disintegrated. Alfred stepped from the licking orange and red flames. He held Alice by the throat. His fingers made indents. Tears streamed down her pale, sooty cheeks.

He lunged forward, but was repelled back by the boundary of the circle. "Let me out!" he raged, eyes alight with fire. "Let me out or I'll rip her to shreds."

"No!" I cried, the terror on Alice's face reflecting my own. I held up the Moldavite skull, which grew hot in my palm. "You hurt her and you'll never get this."

As soon as his eyes snagged on the skull, his grip loosened on Alice and he jerked toward me. "Give me the stone, boy." He held out his hand, just shy of the wall of salt.

"Don't do it." Jason stood beside me, ghost glasses on, Spirit Horn to his ear.

Hannah's EMF detector beeped wildly, and Elena's EVP recorder blinked. Across from me Frank stood still, eyes thoughtful. I knew what I had to do. It was the only way to save Alice. I had to destroy the stone. Destroy his source of power. If he saw me do it, he might lose hope. It'd be dangerous and I'd have to work quickly or he could hurt Alice.

Frank's lips turned up in a tiny quirk, as if he knew what I meant to do, and he gave me a little nod.

I held up the glowing green skull before me as an offering to appease Alfred. "Let her go, and I'll give it to you."

He looked from the stone to Alice and back again, then pulled her closer to him, his massive hands curling into her neck. She cried out in pain.

"I'm no fool, boy. Step inside the circle with the stone. Then I'll release the girl. If not, I'll tear her to shreds." His eyes sparkled with evil glee. "Or what's left of her."

"Don't do it, X." Jason's voice held panic, and I heard Frank ask him exactly what had been said, but I didn't care what Frank thought. Or Jason. Or Hannah. Or Elena. Dangerous or not, I knew what I had to do.

I stepped closer to the circle and raised my foot to step inside.

"Alex, don't." Frank's voice was hoarse with worry.

My eyes flickered up to him. "Trust me." I gave him a little smile and stepped into the salt circle.

Everything moved faster than I could think. Alfred tossed Alice aside and lunged for the stone. She fell to the ashen floor and cried out as her spirit hit the salt. I leapt sideways out of Alfred's grasp, placing myself between him and Alice. In one smooth movement I set the stone skull on the floor before us with my left hand and extended my collapsible escrima stick with my right.

"No!" Alfred screamed, seeming to understand what I was about to do.

I raised the stick high, iron tip pointed at the skull, and brought it crashing down just as Alfred leapt for me.

A brilliant green light exploded from the skull and an ear-bursting crack ripped through the room as I cleaved the skull-shaped stone in two.

Alfred was on his knees before the skull, chest heaving. He clawed at the ashy floor, his hands passing through the skull. His essence was fading. All of the power he'd drawn from the stone was draining away. Just as the skull had lost its power, Alfred was losing his. His spirit dimmed to a translucent form, barely visible. "What have you done?" he moaned.

"It's time, Alfred." He was weakened to the state his spirit had likely been in for the centuries before the skull. I knew the words to help him cross. And this time I spoke them with confidence. *"No matter what you've done or what you fear, spirit, your place to stay is no longer here. Your life and time is now complete. Move into the light that shines before you, then in time you'll be cleansed."*

A vortex of light and dark opened up behind Alfred. I stepped back. Alice clung to my leg in fear. "Don't let him take me," she cried.

I put a gentle hand on her head, but kept my eyes on Alfred. "He's not going to take you, Alice. He's going to where he belongs." I didn't know if he was heading for heaven or hell or someplace in between. Wherever it was, at least he wouldn't be stuck here anymore.

His massive form, illuminated by the light, faded further. Then the last of his rage winked out as he was swallowed up by the twisting tunnel of dark and light.

Then silence. No one stirred. No one made a sound. Only a single cricket somewhere in the rubble chirped out a lonely tune.

I smiled at Alice, but she was gone. But she couldn't have crossed over. Not yet. Could she have been sucked into that swirling vortex with Alfred? No. I'd have seen it. Surely the other side could tell the difference between good and evil.

A whimper and a sniffle made me spin around. I was immediately in Alice's past again. Flames whipped around me, tongues of fire lapped at the ceiling. Yet the fire was no longer hot, the smoke no longer stung my nostrils or made my eyes water. I took three steps toward the massive oak table underneath which Alice had taken shelter in her final minutes. "Alice?"

Nothing.

I squatted down and peered under the table. "Alice." I smiled and held out my hand to the small, burnt girl cowering beneath the false protection of the table. "You can come out now. It's safe."

"Is he gone?" The whites of her eyes glowed through the darkness, illuminated by the ghostly flames. "Truly?"

"He's gone. No one's here but me. You're safe now." I extended my hand, reaching my fingers toward her. "You don't have to do this anymore. Take my hand."

"Uh-uh." She shook her head, eyes downcast.

"Alice," my voice was soft yet firm. "I've never lied to you. I've never hurt you. I'm here to help."

Finally she looked up at me, eyes clouded with doubt. Her chin quivered. "Where will I go?"

My heart ached for her. I couldn't promise her where she would go. I didn't know. All I knew was that my mother had gone somewhere after she'd died. I'd seen her. She was safe and happy and whole. And somehow I knew I'd see her again. "I'm not sure where you'll go."

She scooted backward.

I sighed, keeping my hand outstretched. "But I know my mom is in the light, Alice. She's there and she loves me. She isn't hurt anymore." My voice strangled in my throat at the thought of my mom's accident-broken body, but I shook the thought from my mind. "And I'm sure that's where your parents are, too."

Alice inched her way toward me. "How do you know?"

The fiery, smoky room was turning to ash around us. "Your parents aren't here, Alice. They haven't been here for a very long time. So, they would have crossed over."

"And I'll see them?" she asked, so close to my hand now I could have leaned forward to touch her. But I didn't. She was still afraid, but I needed her to come to me. She had to be open to the idea of leaving or I couldn't help her cross over.

"I believe you will."

"Are you sure?" Her hand hovered above mine, a gentle coolness flowing from her to me.

"Let's go and find them." I wrapped my fingers around hers and she crawled out and stood beside me.

Hand in hand we walked toward the center of the room as I said the prayer of crossing over.

The flames around us died away. They'd been nothing but ghost flames, spirit fire. A memory of the fire that had claimed Alice's life. The café was still a burnt-out, empty shell, but she was safe now.

Before my eyes, Alice's charred skin began to disappear. No longer was she burnt or covered in ash. Her skin was smooth and clean and healed. She lifted her face, mouth open in wonder. "It's so beautiful," she whispered.

I couldn't see the light, but imagined it must be wonderful. "Do you see your parents, Alice?"

Head cocked to one side, she squinted, then a huge, beautiful smile broke out onto her face. "Mama! Papa!"

Alice's hand fell from mine and she ran toward whatever she saw. My heart ached just a little that she hadn't said goodbye; but it wasn't my place to ask for hugs or thanks. It was my job to help spirits move to where they belonged.

Suddenly Alice stopped and turned back toward me. In that moment, I saw her standing with two figures. A man and a woman. The same I'd seen the first time I'd encountered Alice's death. They all smiled at me, and though I could not hear her, Alice's lips moved: "Thank you."

And then, together, they disappeared.

CHAPTER EIGHTEEN

As soon as Alice and her parents had vanished, I was back in my own time. My own reality. Jason had his ghost glasses off and was babbling something at me, and Hannah was following Elena, who was moving toward the voices coming through the half-hinged doors that led to the front of the café.

"Alex," Jason's voice cut through the fog in my brain. "Alex. OPI is here. Are you back yet?"

I shook my head clear of the fuzziness, scooped up the two broken pieces of Moldavite and stowed them in my pocket. A nauseous feeling swirled in my stomach, but quickly faded. Nausea and head fog weren't great, but they didn't last long and were a whole lot better than a headache jackhammering into my brain.

Jason stowed the ghost goggles in the leather pouch he had slung over his shoulder and led the way toward the raucousness of raised adult voices.

Frank stood tall, arms crossed over his chest. Elena stood quietly by. Randle Gallows was there, too, pointing an accusing finger. And some man I didn't recognize was there, too.

"Paranormal investigators, untrained children, working with Psychic Investigators! It's ridiculous! It's a miracle they weren't killed." Gallows's voice echoed through the charred and empty room. "And if they had been, it would be *your* fault!" He stabbed his finger at Frank.

"The OPI has permitted paranormal investigators to work on cases when the Town Psychic isn't available, and recently, as you know, we've been working with PIs on the hospital case."

Gallows made a huffing, seething noise through his nose. "Not on my recommendation, you haven't."

"From what I can tell, you haven't made any recommendations worth using," Frank spat.

Gallows's pale face reddened with rage. But before he could explode, the other man spoke. "I believe we have some new arrivals." He smiled at me and Hannah and Jason. "Why don't we hear what the children have to say about their work with Frank and what they've accomplished?" His voice was calm and patient. Something about him made him seem like a high-ranking person. The boss or something.

He nodded to Elena. "Good to see you, Elena." He smiled, then extended his hand to me, then Hannah and Jason. "I'm Richard Alder, director of the OPI."

"*The* director of the OPI? From Washington, D.C.?" Hannah's eyes were huge behind her glasses like they were going to bug out of her head. Hannah wouldn't go nuts if she met a famous actor; she'd go nuts meeting famous psychic investigators—or the head of the OPI.

Mr. Alder shook her hand with a chuckle. "The very one. I came to see how things were moving along with the hospital haunting, and decided I'd come and meet the famous Alex Lenard."

Me? Famous? I snorted back a laugh. Hardly. "I'm not famous."

"To the world, perhaps not. But to the OPI you are. The first boy to become psychic after age ten. It's never happened before, which is why I gave the approval for Frank to teach you."

So the approval for Frank to teach me had gone all the way up to the top of the OPI. Wow. I hadn't known that. "I—thank you," I stammered.

"Frank tells me you're doing very well, and that you've almost completed all of your basic psychic training."

"I have?" I knew I was close, but I didn't know I was that close. My eyes darted to Frank, who gave me a wide-eyed watch-what-you-say look. "I mean, of course I have. I'm ready to become a fully certified apprentice," I said, my voice confident. That was true. I was ready.

Mr. Alder sniffed. "They're all gone now, haven't they?"

I nodded. "Yes, sir. All of them." I wasn't sure what I should or shouldn't say.

"It's fine, Alex. You can give Richard a full verbal report. He knows we'll send in the official report later." Frank's eyes challenged Randle Gallows, who scowled but said nothing.

So, I told Mr. Alder everything that had happened from the first time I'd seen Alice until I'd finally crossed Alfred over and ultimately helped Alice find peace.

"And where is this stone now?" Mr. Alder asked.

I pulled the two pieces of the green skull from my pocket and held it out. Everyone's eyes were aimed at the stone.

"That could very well be linked with the hospital and the other slew of hauntings we've had around the city," Gallows said. "It could give us valuable clues about what's been happening here."

I nodded. "I think it is."

"And it's likely dangerous," Gallows sputtered. "Another mark against Frank. Letting a young psychic hold on to such a dangerous artifact."

"You're absolutely, right, Randle. It could be a valuable and dangerous piece of evidence," Frank said, making me feel like I had a tiny bomb in my hand.

"Richard," Gallows whined, a desperate plea to his voice. "This is my jurisdiction. Tell them I need the stone to properly research these hauntings."

Mr. Alder appeared to measure each man and his words with his eyes. "You won't lose your position by not having the stone to study, Randle. And we have more forensics equipment in D.C. than you do here. May I see it?" he asked me.

I rolled the pieces over in my hand a couple times and bit my lip, then I pointed out a few of the tiny symbols engraved on the skull. "There are fire sigils. Sigils to raise spirits. Sigils to cause harm," I said, then handed the pieces over to Mr. Alder under Gallows's hungry gaze.

Alder took the small skull pieces from me and turned them over in his hand, squinting at them. Finally, he looked up at me, eyebrows raised. "I recognize some of the symbols, but not all of them. Your apprentice has done his research, it appears. However..." he continued.

Gallows stepped closer, focused on the stone.

Alder gave Gallows a dismissive frown, pulled a small specimen bag from his pocket, and placed the two pieces of the Moldavite inside. "However," he repeated, "this specimen needs to go to our OPI lab in D.C. to be fully studied and documented. And then, yes, it will go into the vaults for safekeeping."

"But—" Gallows looked like a kid who'd just had his cotton candy snatched from him.

"No buts, Randle. You're perfectly capable of handling the hospital outbreak without this." He lifted the bag, then tucked it inside his breast pocket. "And, if we find anything of use once the analysts are finished, I'll be sure you get the report."

"See that you do," Gallows snapped. But a heavy-eyed frown from Richard Alder made him sputter. "Please. That would be most helpful."

Alder nodded, and Gallows took the opportunity to turn and leave.

The room itself seemed to breathe a sigh of relief as Gallows left. Even Mr. Alder seemed lighter.

"I also wanted to tell you that this young lady," Frank put a hand on Hannah's shoulder, "she has captured what I believe is a breakthrough EVP recording."

"Interesting. I'd like to get a copy of it, please," Mr. Alder said to Hannah.

Hannah was speechless for a moment, then seemed to find her words. "I—I need to download it and clean it up, sir, but I'd love for you to hear it."

"As soon as it's ready, have Frank send me a copy."

"Yes, sir." Hannah grinned wider than one of the jack-o'-lanterns in Madame Monique's shop.

"And Alex, since your studies are going so well, and since you"—Mr. Alder smiled and took in all of us—Hannah and Jason, Elena and Frank—"and your team have done an exemplary job with this case, I don't see any reason why you shouldn't keep working together."

Hannah squeaked in excitement, and both she and Jason jumped up and down. Elena grinned, and even Frank couldn't help smiling.

"And," Mr. Alder continued, "since you're caught up with your Elementary Psychic Studies, I don't see any reason why you shouldn't get your final approval as a Certified Apprentice Psychic. Do you, Frank?"

Frank suddenly got serious, and I felt the weight of his mentor stare on me. "Are you ready for that, Alex?"

Was I ready? Well, I knew more advanced wards and sigils than what was in the *Elementary Psychic Studies* books. I'd learned the whole book, cover to cover—mostly. And I had already acted as an Apprentice Psychic on three cases now. So... "Yeah. I mean, yes, sir. I think I am."

Mr. Alder gave a decisive bob of the head and shook my hand again. "Then as soon as Frank gets the paperwork filed, I'll see that it's approved—personally."

It was no one's birthday, but that didn't matter to Hannah or Elena or Mrs. Wilson. Even Jason seemed excited to be having a party.

Elena unveiled a cake in the middle of the table, and Jason gasped. "Is it a piñata cake?" I could almost see the drool dribbling out of his mouth and down his chin.

"It is." Elena smiled. "Hannah and I picked it up from the bakery on our way here."

Jason and I loved piñata cakes. We'd each had one for our tenth birthdays, but nothing since. They were white cake with buttercream frosting, but the inside was hollowed out and filled with sprinkles. So, when you cut into it, a party of sugary color streamed out.

"What are we celebrating again?" I asked, eyeing the massive white cake with multicolored sprinkles in the middle of the table.

"We're celebrating success." Mrs. Wilson floated around happily, setting out plates and napkins and forks and knives.

Merow. Onyx leapt onto the table and sniffed the cake.

"Get down," Mrs. Wilson commanded.

Onyx looked at her, then raised his paw as if he would sample the cake.

"Now," Mrs. Wilson barked.

He dipped his paw in the frosting, took a lick, then sauntered off the table and onto my lap. Frank and I burst out laughing, but Mrs. Wilson frowned.

"That cat..."

"What'd he do?" Jason asked, reaching for the *specula spiritis* case he now wore on him as part of his daily clothing.

"You don't need 'em, J. Onyx just wanted to try a bite of the frosting." I grinned.

Frank settled into a seat beside me. "Yes. Today we are celebrating success for all you've accomplished. Elena is finding her place with the OPI. Hannah, you've learned to run your aunt's store. You had the foresight to bring extra salt even though we didn't know we'd need it. And you captured the best EVP I've ever heard. It will be a breakthrough for PIs."

"And now I understand something," Hannah said with a shy smile. "I can see ghosts. Not like Alex or Jason or you, but I can see them through data. Through their voices and the recordings I get of their energies. I can see them, too."

Frank nodded, and Elena gave her a quick hug. "That you can. And you'll be instrumental in helping PIs work more regularly with psychics. And Jason. You've proven yourself invaluable to Madame Monique and us with your inventiveness."

Madame Monique smiled. "*Oui*. He is my *mon kè*."

Hannah laughed at the nickname, and Jason grinned.

"And Alex," Frank said. "You have come so far in such a short time—"

"I have." I said it almost like a question, but not quite. I knew I had learned a lot super-fast, but there was still so much to learn. "But I still wish we knew who hid the green skull—" Sure, I was sort of proud of myself, but until we knew who planted the green stone or damaged the wards, more mass hauntings were likely to happen.

"I know, but it's okay to celebrate now and again, too," Frank said, then pulled a folded piece of paper from his pocket. "It's not official yet, but you should know because starting tomorrow you and your team will be helping me and Elena with the hospital case." Frank held up the piece of paper and handed it to me. "The paperwork has been sent to the OPI."

I took the paper from him, unfolded it, and read:

This document is to certify that Alexander Lenard has completed his Elementary Psychic Studies with exemplary results. He is, hereby, recommended to be a Certified Apprentice Psychic.

Tears of happiness blurred my vision, but I refused to let them fall. "Thank you, Frank. Thank you."

Jason gave me a sideways hug and grinned. "Congrats, X!"

"Thanks, J." I grinned back.

Jason grabbed a knife, ready to attack. "Now, let's eat cake!"

Everyone did. I hadn't felt this happy since before Mom had died. And while I missed her, I *was* happy. And now I knew for sure, I was definitely home.

GLOSSARY

Apparition: Any type of ghostly figure. There are four types of apparitions including partial, invisible, visible, and solid.

Partial apparitions don't have a complete body showing. You may see a floating head or another body part. They usually fade away quickly.

Invisible apparitions are ghosts that can't be seen with the naked eye. This entity appears only on camera or video and can look like a shadow or be a clear image. Unusually strong Class A Psychics can sometimes catch the outline of invisible apparitions.

Visible apparitions are ghosts that can be seen by the naked eye. They are either transparent or somewhat transparent; psychics may be able to make out certain details such as clothing or other personal items. On rare occasion, an Untouched may catch a glimpse of a visible apparition.

Solid apparitions are less common than the others. They are spirits that appear as a solid apparition and look as real as a living person or animal, and it may be difficult to tell them between a living being until the apparition disappears. These are the most common ghosts to be seen by Untouched.

Apprentice Psychic: A child usually becomes an Apprentice Psychic at age twelve once they've completed their basic psychic studies. When a child becomes a certified Apprentice Psychic, they receive the Fifth Pentacle of the Moon tattoo on the left forearm.

Basic Psychic Studies: Basic psychic studies comprise two years of in-depth study of the Seals of Solomon, the history of the Problem, and basic wards and symbols to defend and protect against ghosts. This course of study normally begins when a child is ten years old and has tested as a psychic. When a child tests as a psychic, they are given a Fourth Pentacle of the Moon tattoo on the right forearm.

Bloody Threat: A drink concocted and served by Madame Monique to repel vampires. It's made of spicy tomato juice with garlic (one can also add colloidal silver).

Clairaudient: A psychic who can hear or perceive sounds, voices, or noise from the spiritual realm.

Clairscent: A psychic who can smell an odor or fragrance that is not in the physical world, but emanates from a spirit or the spirit world.

Clairsentient: A psychic who gathers information by a feeling with the whole body.

Class A Psychics: The strongest psychics belong to this class. They can see, feel, smell, and hear ghosts and other supernatural entities.

Class B Psychics: The second strongest class of psychics. These psychics can either see and feel or hear and feel ghosts, but not both.

Class C Psychic: The weakest class of psychics. Class C Psychics can feel ghosts at times, but they aren't able to see or hear them with any degree of predictability.

Electromagnetic Field (EMF): An electromagnetic field is a physical field produced by electrically charged objects. Electrical currents and living creatures can affect the EMF; however, if a spirit is present, the EMF may be highly charged.

Electronic Voice Phenomena (EVP): Sounds found on electronic recordings interpreted as spirit voices. These voices are not audible to the Untouched or lower-class psychics when they are recorded.

Elementary Psychic Studies: If a child is determined to be psychic, which is usually at age ten, they are sent to psychic schools to study Elementary Psychic Studies for two years. During this course of study, they use the *Elementary Psychic Studies* book, which provides a history of the ghost Problem, in-depth explanations about the Seals of Solomon and how to use them, as well as other useful wards, sigils, and prayers for protection and helping cross over spirits. Upon completion of their basic studies, they are then apprenticed to a Certified Psychic at age twelve.

Escrima Sticks: Thai fighting sticks that are wood-burned with Seals of Solomon and enhanced with black iron paint.

Fifth Pentacle of the Moon: Protects against phantoms of the night, which may cause restless sleep or nightmares. This Seal tattoo is placed on children when they are twelve years old and begin their apprenticeships.

Fourth Pentacle of the Moon: Defends from evil and from any form of injury to body or soul. The Fourth Pentacle of the Moon tattoo is placed on children when they test as psychic (usually at age ten).

Gauss Meter: A scientific instrument that detects waves in the electromagnetic field. This instrument helps paranormal investigators detect the presence of spirits without a psychic present.

Ghost: The apparition of a dead person in the physical world. A spirit.

Ghostball: 1. A ball with sigils that keep a poltergeist trapped inside so it will move on its own; 2. A game, like soccer, but played with a ghostball.

Ghost Hunters: A Psychic's Manual: The definitive work on ghost hunting. It contains everything a Certified Psychic needs to know about catching, stopping, and crossing over spirits, and includes all types of entities. It has been translated into over six hundred languages and is used by psychics and paranormal investigators worldwide.

Ghost Trap (or Spirit Box): An iron box etched with several Seals of Solomon that can be used to temporarily trap a spirit before it can be crossed over.

God's Eye ("Ojo de Dios"): A spiritual object that originated in Mexico. It is made by weaving a design out of colorful yarn on a wooden cross.

Great Unleashing: An event that occurred in 1900 when a group of British and American spiritualists tore a hole in the veil between our world and the spirit world allowing spirits to roam among the living.

Holy Water: Water that has been blessed by clergy and protects the user against evil.

King Solomon: Also named Jedidiah; King Solomon was a wealthy and wise king of Israel who reigned circa 970 to 931 BCE.

Malevolent Spirit: A malevolent spirit is the soul of a human being who had ill intentions while living. Since spirits retain the same personalities they had while alive, these spirits can be angry, troublesome, and just plain nasty.

Nazar Boncuğu: A brilliant blue eye-shaped amulet, traditional in Turkey, which protects against "the evil eye."

Office of Psychic Education (OPE): The federal organization in the United States of America that oversees the testing, education, and training of psychics.

Office of Psychic Investigation (OPI): The federal organization in the United States of America that defends the country and its citizens against paranormal attacks. There are federal, state, and city offices of the OPI.

Paranormal Cybersecurity Squad (PCS): A federal organization that monitors all electronics in the United States to aid in the prevention of paranormal cyber and electronic attacks.

Paranormal Investigator (PI): Usually an Untouched or someone with little psychic ability who investigates paranormal activity.

Parascope: The Parascope is a triboelectric field meter. It visually indicates static electricity fields vertically with colored lights to give the investigator an idea of which direction the field is traveling.

Pentacle: A talisman or magical object, typically disk-shaped and inscribed with a pentagram (a five-pointed star). A pentacle can sometimes be found in the Seals of Solomon, which wards against evil spirits.

Poltergeist: A supernatural being of unknown origin responsible for loud noises and throwing objects around.

Pretender: An Untouched (nonpsychic) who so desperately wants to be psychic that they pretend to be one.

Renovation Ghost: Ghosts that are tied to a specific building or the land itself. They appear when a home or business has just been built or soon after renovations have occurred.

Residual Haunting: An event or emotional energy from the past that is repeated over and over again as if in a loop. No entity is present.

Seal of Solomon: The legend of the Seal of Solomon is that the ring was engraved by God and was given to the king directly from heaven. There are forty-four Seals of Solomon, some of which can be used for protection against evil.

Shrieking OJ: A concoction created by Madame Monique to protect against ghosts (it's also good for the immune system). It contains orange juice with an iron boost.

Sigil: An inscribed or painted symbol that contains magical power. Often used to keep ghosts and spirits out of homes, offices, schools, etc.

Spellguard: The safest electrical wristwatch on the planet with sigils inscribed on every gear and battery. It also has a nearly invisible seal on the face and a seal and numbers that glow in the dark.

Spirit Horn: A modified form of the Victorian ear trumpet, which is used to help Untouched or psychics without the gift of clairaudience hear ghosts.

Specula spiritis: An invention created by Madame Monique. These "ghost glasses" use ancient symbols and engineering to allow nonpsychics to get a glimpse of the spirit world.

Telepathy: The ability to communicate thoughts and ideas through the mind.

The Problem: The Problem is that ghosts and spirits roam freely in the world of the living. It started when the Victorian spiritualists opened the door from the world of the dead to the world of the living and allowed ghosts and other supernatural beings to roam. They were unable to close the door they opened.

The Sight: The Sight is an extremely rare gift among psychics. It allows them to see the past as if they are the ghost themselves. It often causes the psychic to see or relive the time surrounding the death of the spirit with whom they are interacting. A psychic with the Sight is known as a Seer.

The Stinger: Another drink concocted by Madame Monique to remove curses and protect the person who drinks it from evil. This beverage is made with cranberry juice and stinging nettle.

Third Pentacle of Jupiter: One of the Seals of Solomon. This seal defends and protects those who encounter spirits.

Town Psychic: Local psychics, usually operated by Class B or Class C Psychics, not directly regulated by the OPI. The Town Psychics work out of Town Psychics' Offices and take smaller cases that the local or federal OPI offices are too busy to handle.

Untouched: A nonpsychic person. The Untouched make up roughly 96 percent of the entire living population.

Ward: A type of magic or spell intended to deflect harm or evil.

WardWing: A watch with hands that look like miniature wings and Seals of Solomon interspersed throughout the numbers to protect against any hitchhiking ghosts.

Susan McCauley

Acknowledgements

Thank you, readers, for reading Book 3 of the Ghost Hunters series; I hope you enjoyed a spooky-fun time! Your support is truly appreciated.

I must also thank my fabulous editor, Deborah Halverson, who has supported and encouraged me through my journey of writing of Ghost Hunters: Spirit Fire (and beyond). Thank you to Dan Janeck for his brilliant copyediting skills. Thanks also to the cover illustrator, Bill Ferguson; the art director, Bruce Foster; and the cover designer, Christian Bentulan, for their wonderful cover work. Thank you to Christopher D. Morgan for his beautiful interior layouts.

Thanks to Pat Cuchens, my sweet friend and grammar guru, who catches lots of my typos and grammar snafus, and who lends her emotional support whenever I need it; to the fabulous T. J. Resler, who writes amazing National Geographic books for kids and makes writing conferences so much fun. Thank you to my crazy, fun friends, Melynda Grimes and Kaitlin Burks, for helping me with some of the odds and ends of the business. Also, thank you to my friends at the Horror Writers Association (HWA) and the Society of Children's Book

Writers and Illustrators (SCBWI) for supporting and encouraging me and so many writers. And thanks to all of my family and friends who have believed in me and my writing over the years.

A special thank-you to Fire Chief Michael Hanuscin for generously sharing his firefighting experiences and fire expertise to ensure I got things right in the fire arena. And merci to Audrey Guinaudeau for helping ensure I didn't slaughter the bits of French in this book!

Finally, thank you to my mother, Sandy Basso, who reads and gives me feedback on everything I write; I don't know what I would do without you. And, last, but certainly not least, thank you to my husband, Rick, and my son, Alex, who support me through the ups and downs of the writing process, have patience when I have to write despite them wanting me to do something else, and for their endless love and support.

About the Author

Susan McCauley has been intrigued by ghost stories since she was first enchanted and scared witless on Disney's Haunted Mansion ride at the age of three. She now writes works of horror, paranormal, and dark fantasy (with a particular fondness for ghost stories). She lives in Houston, Texas with her husband, son, three crazy cats, and a wide variety of other pets.

To get the latest news, check out www.sbmccauley.com or connect with her on social media.

If you enjoyed this book, please leave a review with your favorite book retailer, on Goodreads, or both—it will be immensely appreciated!

Spirit Fire

·OTHER BOOKS

72255411R00149